Tales of Shadow Street
Book One

Denise Vitola

&

Morgan Ashe

Copyright

Tales of Shadow Street: Book One
Copyright © 2015 by Shadow Street Press, LLC
ISBN: 978-1-61877-158-2
Cover Artist DarkAshe Graphics

This book is a work of fiction. The names, characters, places, and incidents are products of the writer's imagination or have been used fictitiously and are not to be construed as real. Any resemblance to persons, living or dead, actual events, locale or organizations is entirely coincidental. The publisher does not have any control over and does not assume any responsibility for author or third-party Web sites or their content.

Published in the United States of America
First electronic edition: July 2015 by Shadow Street Press, LLC
First print edition: August 2015 by Shadow Street Press, LLC

DEDICATION

To all the freaks, half-breeds, and undesirables—including us.
Shadow Street is our safe haven.

.

CONTENTS

WELCOME TO SHADOW STREET

Shadow Street is an enigma. Our little slice of paradise can be found in a time slip formed within the Earth Dimension after the Great Splintering. It's called Shadow Street instead of Shadow City, because one of the Guardians of Eternity referred to it by its Latin name—*Umbra Urbis*. (Guardians are hoity-toity and like to make things difficult for all of us.) When Jostun Tipwiller created an original map for the area, he had no idea what *Urbis* meant, so he just called it Shadow Street.

Regardless of the name, it is a place of secrets, of magic, and yes, of mayhem. People live full lives, and by people, I mean Angels, Immortals, Humans, Supernaturals, and Hybrids. Still, there's always trouble when you deal with the likes of sweet-natured Hellhounds and the smoky goodness of *Fumi*. Situations tend to get dicey during the plane shifts with a lot of arguing and moaning about location, location, location. To make matters worse, things get really crazy during those days when both of our moons rise at the same time.

I'd like to say the problems on Shadow Street are easily handled, but the truth of the matter is this—there is a sinister side, and the danger is life-threatening. When the Great Splintering occurred, nine dimensions were formed. One of these planes is home to Lumiel and his Infernal beings, a place so evil that even the worst of the worst try to avoid it. We're linked to the Nine Dimensions by Gates, and as you might guess, the seals on said Gates don't always work. That's when the nasty stuff can happen.

Here you'll find the stories of Shadow Street—the laughter, the love, the deceit, the anguish. You'll meet people who will figuratively steal your heart and those who will, literally, steal your heart. Do be careful as you read. The magic is unpredictable.

You should also know that some of the stories have appeared in other books and on the Internet, but after talking with the folks who were featured therein, we have gained their permission to add the secrets that we left out the first time.

Plus, we never change the names to protect the innocent.

Welcome to Shadow Street.

Thomas, Angel

Part I

Where We Are Now

THE CHIMERA GATE
The Old Quarter
by Denise Vitola

"This is the fifth cold one in the past two weeks," Death said. "I thought I'd better get you."

I nodded and hunkered down, staring at the dead Angel. It was something you didn't see much. We're a hard species to kill, but this one was as clobbered up as they come. His wings were crumpled, but they were white, which meant he was a Pearl—one of Archangel Michael's minions. I could understand if he were a Slate, like me, with nice gray wings, or even a demonic Leatherwing. We're the Angels who frequent Shadow Street, and I was the Angel in charge, the Governor, when it came to reporting to the Guardians of Eternity. Figuratively speaking, the doors are locked, the Crossroads warded. No one was getting in or out without my knowledge, but here he was, which did a little more than annoy me.

Death leaned down and flicked at the plain gold locket the Angel wore. "Do you recognize him?"

"No. I didn't get word that a portal had been opened. My bracelet didn't even go off."

"Maybe he came in a side door, slipped in through a gate. That one over in the Old Quarter, the Chimera, has been leaking, so I understand."

I shook my head, glancing at him. "You said four other folks came up dead?"

"Yeah. They weren't on my dispatch list either. I was called after the fact." He stood, straightened his leather bomber jacket, and smoothed down his jeans. Death had shucked his grim reaper style for a Human look. It suited him.

"I know you like to stay loose and not get involved, but we have a serial killer here. The Guardians are going to get wind of this soon. Better you know about it and put an end to this madness before they come up with their crooks and wands and bad attitudes."

"Who else have you found lying around dead?"

"The butcher, a vamp, a mage—Old Herman, in fact—and Dr. Goodman."

"Herman? I just saw him in the Gargoyle's Perch a few nights ago."

"Yeah, he kicked off after he left the pub. Found him belly-up in the alley next door. No sign of attack. Just like the others. I'd say natural causes, but vamps have never been part of that equation."

"Who told you about this?"

"Actually, Beka got a report from one of her lookouts."

Beka was the person in charge of the Shadow Keepers, a group of supernatural folks who had their ears to the ground on Shadow Street. She was also Death's Human girlfriend and if it could be said, Mr. D. was mad about her. She was his one passion in an immortal life.

I studied the Angel. He had that androgynous look so favored by the Pearl echelon of Angels. No beard, not even stubble. A straight nose. Thin lips. A diamond stud in his left ear. Hands that were soft looking with long fingers. He wore a white shirt that was unstained. Of course, a Pearl's blood was clear, so unless I undressed him, I wouldn't find a wound. His pants were white, too—a fashion faux pas this long after Labor Day. His shoes were missing, and he had charming toenails painted in white glittery polish. Something occurred to me as I stared at those girly nails. I reached forward to press the palm of my hand against his chest. When I did, my breath caught.

Holy *Santa Muerte*. This cat no longer had his Angelic essence. It was gone. No lingering tendrils of grace or supernatural ego, no connection to the Angelic Realm. Nothing. He was as vacant as a ghost's eye.

Among the mortals, there are several theories of how the multi-dimensional universe came into being. They quantum mechanic the hell out of it, add silly putty and string theory, but really, it had nothing to do with atoms or quarks and everything to do with Lumiel and Apollyon.

These two were as bad as they came. Twins, which is a rarity among Angels, but not unheard. Both wanted to rule everything—Earth, Heaven, and anything else they could get their hands on.

The two had a terrible row involving swords of light and darkness. Lumiel always thought he would have the upper hand, but Apollyon was certain he would win. Their battle was so horrific that it shook the very columns that supported the Universe and no one dared to intervene, even Michael or Zeus. When all was said and done, there was a humongous implosion—and the Universe fractured into nine dimensions. Most of us clung to the luminescent dimension. Shadow Street was created as a pocket dimension of Earth, a time slip, if you will.

Lumiel tumbled into the Ninth Dimension, along with all of his Infernals. He resides there to this day, his Legion causing havoc and hatred throughout the other planes of existence. As for Apollyon? No one knows for sure what happened to him. He may have been swallowed by the expanse of dark matter after the implosion, but then again, maybe not. One thing is for certain, though.

We haven't seen the last of that demon, not by a long shot.

The first thing I did was to head over to the You Stab 'Em, We Slab 'Em Medical Examiner's Office. I found Wiley Sykes eating a sandwich while he autopsied Ren Hildalgo, our ancient, but now quite dead of natural causes, Kun. Kuns were giant fish that turned into giant birds or maybe they were giant birds that turned into giant fish—I was never clear on that point. Either way, she was both scale and feather lying atop the exam table.

Wiley Sykes was a gnome with a bad attitude. His bushy eyebrows were always in a bunch from the deep frown he wore on his pink-skinned face. He was a barrel-chested fellow with skinny legs and arms, but he had a powerful strength that was the hallmark of his species. I'd seen him flop bodies on the table by himself. He stood on a box, glaring at me for interrupting him.

"I was wondering when you'd get yourself over here," he said in that high, squeaky voice that made me sweat behind the eyeballs. "You haven't been paying attention, Thomas."

"Is it so hard for folks to think that I have a life?" I asked. "I spent a few days at the RiverSide House with my girl." What I didn't mention was that all that fun we had took the energy right out of me, and I'd returned to my place to sleep for a day and a half.

"Oh, that's why the Neph's tattoo shop was closed."

"Wiley, I'm not here to talk about my relationship with Esa."

"Aye, you want to know about the murders. Well, I can't tell you much."

"Why not?"

"Because other than the vamp, they all died of natural causes as far as I can tell. The vamp had her head cut off, but for a vamp, that is a natural cause, I suppose."

He took a huge bite of sandwich, and I smelled the acrid scent of banana peppers. He chewed the bite thoughtfully before answering me. "Okay, to be more specific, what must have killed them was a supernatural cause that doesn't show up in the natural theater of medical science." Wiley took another bite, chewed, and then explained. "The Butcher had fat around his heart, but that didn't kill him, Old Herman was especially spry for being two-hundred-years old, and Doc Goodwin had a bit of frost on his lungs from smoking those damned Khohls, but that's not what killed him. I just couldn't find a definitive cause of death on any of them. Except the vamp."

"Are there crime scene reports?"

"With our cops?" He guffawed, and it was an odd sound with his high-pitched voice. "Naw, not beyond making an initial report of finding a body in the alley. No disturbances in the areas where they were found. Since Shadow Street doesn't have a forensics division, we have to eyeball the stuff, and that method doesn't give us many clues. Besides, the cops aren't going to disturb their donut breaks for what is strange, but resolvable. Judge Roy Bean has been on a fishing trip at the River Lethe, so good luck getting him up to speed. It'll take a month for the forgetfulness to leave his brain. Why the hell would you cast a line there knowing how potent that water is?"

"I hear the trout are good, and folks want to forget their troubles. Two vacations at once." I stared at Ren, but my mind flowed to other things. "Did you talk to Chief Claudia?"

"When I reported that they died of natural causes, it was case closed. It's probably why she didn't contact you."

The reason the Chief of Police didn't contact me was because she was useless. I wouldn't get any info from her, no matter what I did even if I could find her, which wouldn't be easy with her being part Ahool. I decided not to waste my time.

I nodded toward Wiley. "You dropped some of your sandwich inside the corpse."

He glanced down, and his eyebrows knitted even closer. "Dang it." He reached inside the body opening to extract a piece of onion. "Oh, well, these things give me indigestion anyway."

The pocket dimension that encompasses Shadow Street also encompasses other encampments in our pockmarked landscape. Down the road a piece and back through time, the Guardians of Eternity chiseled out a hallowed hall so that they could keep administrating the Earth Dimension. Lumiel, the monster of Perdition, had placed himself in charge of the other nine planes, and you can be sure he didn't do it by democratic vote. He is an unholy monster when it comes to any interference in his realm and the immortal parliament lets him be so long as he stays on his side of the line.

All the gods of Earth's history have carved out an Elysian Fields Old Folks Home where they bide their days playing *bocce*, giving each other back rubs, and taking luxury cruises to the planet to cause havoc and regret wherever they can. Half the Guardians are elder gods—Odin, Zeus, Isis— folks who can be fair and just when they want to be and downright mean when they don't. We Angels tend to talk them down a whole lot, because we're as old and as immortal as they are. Granted, most of us carry our own curses, and we're not immune to the mutable. What's that saying? Shit Happens.

It certainly does.

I stopped by the Shadow Street Mortuary and checked out the bodies being dressed for burial at the Whisper Cemetery. The Mortician assistant and cosmetologist, Mildred Sparks, was fiddling and fooling with the body of the vamp. I don't care how good you are with the war paints, making a decapitated head look like it was still part of a body was a mean trick. Mildred prided herself on never using beauty spells and, even when under deadline, she insisted on getting out the eyebrow pencil for touch-ups. She sat there listening to rap music on the radio while she pushed the ookey ends together and hid them with a designer scarf.

As I said, Shadow Street is contained in a pocket dimension, a time slip, if you will. This is the place that the Guardians of Eternity send people who are free thinkers, bad apples, and just plain pain in the asses to the *status quo*. I was here as the Governor to make sure things went smoothly, but even I was not immune to this prison. I'd pissed off Archangel Michael one too many times and now I paid for it with this assignment. I had news for them, though. I liked it here.

Had I not seen her file, I would never have guessed what Mildred was in for. There had been a time when she'd abused her witching powers. She'd owned her own beauty salon and if a woman crossed her in some way, she'd turn their faces into meat pies with the dark unguents she marketed as face creams. When she came to Shadow Street, she'd tried to get a job at the local hair salon, but the answer had been no, so she did the next best thing and turned to mortuary work. Now Mildred was a supernatural teetotaler, getting her kicks with make-up and curlers. Plus, the dead never talked back.

She smiled when she saw me, drawing up her fat red lips set in a jowly face. Running a hand through her bleached blond hair, she patted a wayward wave into place. She smelled like cigarettes and cheap perfume. Her blue smock was smudged with the rainbow of colored powders she used to soften the impact of her make-up statement. I could see a ruffled collar rising above the neck of her smock and noticed the edge of a large brass locket peeking out between the space of missed buttons. Mildred noticed me looking at it, and self-consciously nested it inside her blouse and into the groove between her ample breasts.

"Why, if it isn't the Angel Thomas," she cooed. "I was wondering when you might show up." She swiveled in her chair to turn the radio off. "I suppose you're here about this one."

"Her and the four others you've worked on this week."

"She's all I've got left. The others are in the ground already, but we had to wait for the nightside for all the vamps to come to her funeral."

"What's her name?"

"Shelia Van Twern." Mildred pushed up a curl along the vamp's cheek. "These creatures have hair like straw. Can't do much with it."

"Did you notice if she had any unusual tattoos?"

"She's loaded with them." Mildred scooted up the sleeve on the dress, showing me a forearm decorated from elbow to fingertip. "Miss Van Twern has them all over her body like this. They stop at the neckline and the ankles."

"I'm looking for a particular one." I rolled up my sleeve. "Like this one."

Mildred thought a moment. "An ouroboros?"

"It is. Granted by the Guardians for a specific reason."

"Are there many around who have this mark?"

I shook my head. "No, just a few as far as I know, but the Guardians don't tell me everything."

Mildred dabbed a bit of blush on Miss Van Twern's cheek. "I'd remember seeing that. No, she just has the usual funky crap that vamps seem to love."

"What about the others? Did you notice it on them?"

She stared at me longer than she should have. "What's so special about the tattoo, Thomas?"

I shrugged. "Just trying to find a connection is all. Serial killers usually hone in on some feature of their victim."

"Well, I can truly say, they were as bald as babies. Haven't seen the Angel yet, though."

"How did you know about that? They just found him."

She smiled. "Word travels fast, and old Maury takes his mortuary business seriously."

"But, he's an Angel. He's ascended, so he won't be coming through here. His body has probably turned to ash."

"Oh, well, then, I guess I won't get a look, now will I?"

I nodded. "I need to touch her. May I, Mildred?"

"Why, of course. You're the Governor. I couldn't deny you even if I wanted to. Sure don't want it getting back to the Guardians that I was uncooperative."

"I'd never speak ill of you, Mildred," I answered, with a grin. "Who would doll up our dead?"

She smiled. "See, that's what I say."

I leaned over and studied the vamp. Miss Van Twern had obviously been turned late in life, because not even Mildred's ministrations could hide the fact that she was one old broad. Her skin sat loose along her neck, and her hands were gnarled with age.

"You know, she was a hooker," Mildred said, just as I reached my hand out.

Her words stopped me in my tracks. "Independent?"

"I suppose," she answered. "There is something else you might be interested in."

"What's that?"

"They all knew each other. All the victims. Except maybe the Angel. I never saw them talking to wingers. But the ones who passed through here were drinking buddies down at the Gargoyle Perch. Of course, Old Doc Goodman would drink with anybody." She paused to laugh. "Old scudder. Used to try to put the make on me every time I showed up for a nightcap. Anyway, I'd see them sitting together." She pointed to the vamp. "Even her. My guess is they got into something with the gang of Moon Fae that just came in. Those folks don't play games when it comes to glamouring folks."

No, they didn't. But the Moon Fae didn't play during the day plane, so they couldn't have killed the others. Still, they had their minions. "Thank you for that information, Mildred. I'll remember how cooperative you were in this investigation."

She cooed and blinked as I touched the vamp. Nothing. Empty. No lingering wisps of essence.

When Shadow Street was formed, we ended up with two moons. They are known as the Dusky Moon and the Sparkling Moon. These two moons control what are known as shifts. When the Dusky Moon rises and stays in the sky for an earthtime month, the world exists in perpetual night. When it sets, the Sparkling Moon rises and then we get an approximation of daylight, a bit gloomy, but light enough to read by. We do have weather, in case you are wondering, rain and wind. There are seasons, too, thanks to the Goddess Demeter, but you would never really know it. As Edgar Allan Poe once remarked when he visited here, "It's like the October of my most memorable year." Suffice it to say, you need to wear a coat on most days.

Most times are like this, safe and easy, but four times a year, we have perigee, when both moons are so close that they rise together. We call it the Kissing Moons. It's a time of uncertainty, fear, and wonton disregard for the few laws we have here. So like any society, when the satellites almost collide, we hold festivals.

We Angels can do a lot. We can fly, time travel, deliver miracles, and squeeze a thousand of us onto the head of a pin. We can also make likeness of things we see by touching our hands to a blank piece of paper, parchment, wood, or fabric. This is exactly what I did when Dicky, the owner of the Gargoyle Perch Pub, asked me if I wanted a drink. I chose a durian-flavored beer, placed the palms of my hands onto his sparkling bar and realized the picture of the dead Angel.

Dicky looked appalled until I told him the picture would fade in a minute or two.

He studied the likeness and then poured off my draft, using a stick emblazoned with a silver gargoyle whose eyes lit red when the beer spilled into the glass. He slid the tankard over the face of the Angel. Dicky was a taciturn shapeshifter, prone to using baseball bats when folks started acting up in his pub. He'd come to Shadow Street because that same Louisville Slugger had severely dented an irate customer in the tavern he used to own in Pittsburgh. He didn't much care for Shadow Street, but the authorities couldn't hold him, because he kept turning into a Sasquatch and bending the bars on cells or smashing the unsmashable doors to the lockup.

Dicky nodded, scraping a hand against his perfectly bald head. "I seen him. He was here last night raisin' hell."

"What was his bitch?" I asked.

Dicky studied me, and I realized that in his Human form, he had a crooked nose. "Don't you know?"

I took a long sniff of the beer and smelled the manure scent of the durian fruit that had helped to create the most iconic beer on Shadow Street. It smelled like shit, but had a sweet taste in the back of the throat that reminded me of the water in Heaven on a Tuesday night. I slugged the beer and wiped my mouth with the back of my hand. "If I did, I wouldn't have asked you."

"He said he was here to take your place."

"My place? That's news to me."

"Said he was going to clean up Shadow Street, because you were a lazy no-gooder and Archangel Michael had enough of the bottom feeders getting their way here."

"Was this the first time he'd been in your place?"

"Yep. Never saw him afore last night. Said he'd just arrived after having cleaned up the City of Dis." He snorted. "Like that den of Iniquity could ever be cleaned up. I knew he was a liar the moment he made that claim. I been to Dis. The Guardians tried to lock me up there, but I made such a stink that even the demons didn't want me." He barked, which was Dicky's way of laughing sardonically.

Dis was a city of dark spirits, and it existed on the seventh circle of Hell. A Pearl would never venture there, because the Leather Wings would rip him to shreds. They didn't like Pearls and Slates impinging on their territory. I can't blame them. They did things their way with violent intent.

Pearls were goody-two-shoes, and we Slates fell somewhere in between—addicted to Human vices and a wee bit nasty-mean on occasion, but usually nice enough Joes to be around on a daily basis.

Dicky wiped at the picture on his bar with a wet rag. "Folks was gettin' riled up, so I put on my muscles by shifting into my alter ego and threw his ass out the door."

"What time was that?"

"About 1 a.m., I think. Didn't look at the clock." He pointed to my glass. "You want another?"

"Yeah. Was he picking on anyone in particular, or was he just talking out loud?"

"Well, Gim LaPork was here, and he was pissed off what with his pa getting whacked and all."

"What did he do?"

"He threatened to wring the Angel's neck like a chicken if he kept talking mean about you." He shoved a fresh glass my way. "You got a real fan in that family."

"Melk was the best butcher on Shadow Street. I buy all my meat from the LaPorks." I took another hardy swig. "Did they go to fisticuffs?"

"No, I pushed the Angel out the door. Of course, Gim left about five minutes later, so I don't know where or what he did. Why?"

"We found the Angel dead this morning."

Dicky blinked at me, and I swear he looked more Bigfoot than Human at that moment. "If that don't beat all. You folks can die?"

"We ascend, which is a bit different. You might say we enter Heaven by the back door." What I didn't tell him was that Angels also recycled. New wings, new bodies, new desires. Same old bad habits, but Pearls were squeaky clean, so bad habits and bragging seemed out of character. Now,

15

self-righteous bullshit? That was more a Pearl's stock and trade. "Was he in here drinking?"

"He had a light beer," Dicky said, adding a chuckle. "Turned his nose up at the Durian. Pussy."

I almost didn't hide my smile. "What was the last straw?"

"He said he had the power to take any one of us outta Shadow Street and back to Earth. All we had to do was pay up."

"Pay up?"

"Lick his toes, you know? Well, folks 'round these parts don't take kindly to that. We may be the dregs, but that's just what the Guardians think. We got self-respect. It's about all we got. Not none of us would lower ourselves for such as him. We'd do *you* a favor, because you do us favors. But not him." Dicky mopped up the bar, concentrating on a speck of dirt in front of me that even with my Angel eyes I couldn't see. "I don't think Gim had anything to do with it," he continued, absently. "I sure hope not, anyway. I don't like the thought that we might not be able to get fresh meat delivered in if he did. This place is always going to need a butcher since there's all them Carnivores living down by the river. Melk had good contacts on the Earth plane, and he never tried to jump ship and leave us high and dry for someplace better than Shadow Street. He was a family man what cared about his community."

I nodded and polished off my drink. The thing about that was—supplies could come in, but leaving was another matter altogether.

Shadow Street is so situated that when the moons rise, we shift in physicality. There are day businesses and night business and some, like the Shadow Street Diner, that overlapped between them. Most merchants have two addresses for the same shop to accommodate the shifts. Alleyway entrances change, main street doors fade to invisible, and walls rearrange. Street lights change directions and corners straighten out. Houses and apartment tenements divide and multiply. It's like an Escher painting on steroids, but people consigned to this pocket dimension are each gifted with an internal GPS before being dropped into this world. Without this guidance system, most people would surely lose their minds when trying to bridge day and night. When I say most people, I'm not talking about Angels. We were created with these compasses, like birds that can migrate north each year by following the lay lines of Earth's magnetism.

It was noon on the dark plane and the Dusky Moon was high in the sky as I stepped out onto the street. I was met and greeted by many folks who rarely ventured out during the day plane. Vamps, Weres, Fae, Ghouls, Amaroks—even a few Will-o'-Wisps and a couple of Kitsune—a husband and wife team who loved practical jokes. Everyone pasted on a smile when they saw me walking their way, whether they felt the pleasure or not. I was the most agreeable Governor among the many who had passed through Shadow Street, and they were going to do their best to make sure I stayed. Little did they know that I wasn't going anywhere for a long time. Not only was I born with that GPS, the Guardians had made sure I'd been installed with a tracker, so if I left for any length of time, they knew where to find me and call me back home.

I'd come to Shadow Street because the Guardians felt I'd been too free with knowledge for mortals, among other things. Humans and their various hybrid brothers were species created to populate worlds where resources were outstanding, but sentient slaves were in short supply. Humanity stretched all across the regional galactic arm, doing the bidding of masters that kept them firmly in tow. It was only on Earth that mortals could self-actualize and that was thanks to me and few other Angels. We'd had a beef early on with reasons for breeding folks and then not giving them a say in their lives. Of course, most mortals in the Earth plane had no clue that their day-to-day affairs, coincidences, miracles, fights, wars, arguments, and lovemaking were all planned out on a cosmic spreadsheet. Still, the fact that they could read, write, cypher, and fly to the moon made it at least a bearable affair.

The night plane always appeals to me better than the day plane. I like shadows and Shadow People, because, like me, they are misunderstood. Miracles often take place in the dark recesses of understanding. Shadow People are usually behind them, even though they have spun this appalling propaganda that they are evil incarnate. I think it's the glowing red eyes that do it. Still, if you have a Shadow Person dogging your trail, then something good will come out of it.

And that's what I needed right now—a minor miracle to solve this case. Sleuthing wasn't my favorite pastime. I got my jollies by interfering in peoples' lives—mostly for the good, some for the bad—especially when they twisted my feathers the wrong way. This killer was going down when I finally ran across him.

I found Gim's butcher shop, No Pork Chops, situated between the Shadow Street Diner and the Bare and Claw Strip Club. During the day plane, No Pork Chops kept a proud spot at the only entrance to the rambling expanse of the Moonlight Market. When the night plane shifted, Melk would bitch continually about how he was forced to endure strippers smelling of raunchy perfume and the diner smelling of bacon grease. He'd grumble about the loathsome smell, but Sal, the owner of the diner, told him that folks preferred the real thing to that stuff made from turkey and tofu. You may guess that there was a constant barrage of insults and invectives hurled during the night plane shop shift.

I entered the store, hanging back for a bit, because the place was crowded. Festival Days were coming and folks were sourcing food as well as goodies for prezzies. No Pork Chops was the first stop most people made because of LaPork's Famous Festival Stew, made with lots of Burgundy wine, pearl onions, carrots, and the best cuts of beef. When the place thinned out, I approached the girl behind the counter. She was a hybrid, too, but she looked a bit like a goose with her long neck. She even honked when she talked, pointing behind the counter to the solitary office wedged between the loading dock and the freezer. I swept on through as the front door opened to let in a new hoard of shoppers.

Gim was the spitting image of Melk. Big, burly, fat, and with a porcine nose and tiny eyes. His ears flopped down over his round head, and when he smiled, I saw delicate canine teeth. He had been sitting behind a worn desk, punching numbers into an old printing calculator. How he managed it with three fingers that ended in hoofs was beyond me. He shook my hand, pointing to a filthy chair. I sat—glad I wore jeans.

"I suppose you're here about me dad," he lisped.

"Can you tell me about his movements that last day?" I asked.

"I'd like to say it was the usual, you know? But it weren't. Me dad was expectin' a brand new load of Kobi beef. We haven't ever gotten that here on Shadow Street. Some supplier in Japan was tryin' to unload it. Called it Fukushima Prime. Dad was like a little piglet at the Feast of St. Isadore the Farmer. He couldn't believe his good luck at getting such a deal."

Holy Three-Eyed Fish. The Fukushima-Daichi Nuclear Plant still spilled radioactive crap into the Pacific and there was a 20-mile uninhabited zone around it. "Did you ever get that delivery?"

"No. Me dad never made it to the pickup portal."

Thank the Forces that Be. I made a mental note to talk to Michael about that. We were prisoners of sorts, but not death row inmates. "Tell me what happened."

Gim gathered up a painful look on his piggy face. "Someone jumped him as he was leavin' the gate. Must have been more than one person or someone with damned powerful magic to bring down me dad. He weighed almost 500 pounds. Dragged him into an alley and slit his throat from jowl to jowl." He shook his head. "No better than slaughterin' a goat."

"Did anyone see anything? What about the cops?"

"Well, off the record and I hope this don't make ya fluff up with anger, but them cops ain't no use at all. They didn't see nothin'. So they said. Humans what turn a blind eye unless ya got some smart bills to press to their palms. We're supposed to be the scum of the world, so what does that make them?"

"No better than we are." I rolled up my sleeve and showed him my tattoo. "Your dad or you have this mark?"

Gim glanced at it. "Naw. We don't go in for that stuff. Come into this world pink. Go out the same way."

Shadow Street's time slip is connected to Earth by portals. There are specific juncture boxes—some placed in the broom and mop closets of the shops, some hidden in the recesses of corner prayer altars, and some in houses and public buildings. The Elysian Fields Old Folks Home has one and there is one at the back of the Shadow Street souk known as the Moonlight Market where food and supply deliveries are made to the various retailers. The boxes hold a redundancy, of course, so not just anyone can access the portals. You need a special bracelet that holds the combination to the box and then, only certain folks are entrusted with the bracelets.

Folks like Death have a combo to the Afterlife Portal so he can ferry mortals and their souls into the Dimension of Shades. The owner of the Moonlight Market has one, of course, and folks like Judge Roy Bean keep a bracelet, as does Dr. Frankenstein, since he is the administrator of the hospital and needs medical supplies. Me? I have all the keys. Not only do I have a jingly charm bracelet, I also have the key that accesses the gates.

If I ever get mugged, it's going to be a hell of a payday for someone.

When I left Gim's place, I happened to glance over at the diner and saw Death and his gal, Beka, through the window. They had that slobbering Hellhound with them and all three were wolfing down pancakes. Watching them, I realized I was a bit peckish myself, so I sauntered in.

The diner was modeled after the rail car diners of the 1920s and '30s America. It was chrome and red Formica. The cook and owner, a reed thin Human named Sal, worked in the galley behind the counter. All you could see of him through the narrow window beyond the stacked up dishes waiting for service was his intent expression and the fact that he sweated like he tended a real train stove.

Death saw me and waved me over.

"Join us, won't you?" Beka asked.

She was a real looker. Just barely legal with a body and face to make the men swoon, she was combat ready dressed in camos and a tight black sweater, yet feminine by sporting a pair of hand knit wristlets with beads and frilly edges. Beka's thick black hair was pulled into a French twist and doffed with a sprig of lavender. She was the new head of the Shadow Keepers, a group who kept the really undesirable folks in check. That oversight included the cops, because not a one sent here had any redeeming values, and that included the chief. Beka was a native to Shadow Street, born and bred in this pocket dimension without any clue what it was like to live Earthside. There were more and more children of Shadow Street, but when they reached the age of majority, and dependent upon how well they had acted during their formative years, they were given the opportunity for truancy. Most left Shadow Street and never came back. I blame it on real sunshine and Florida weather.

The funny thing was that despite being drop-dead gorgeous, no one could get near Beka—not because of Death's vigilance, but that of the Hellhound. She glanced at the creature of the underworld with a loving look on her face. "Smokie, you need to get down now and let the nice Angel slide into the booth."

Smokie gave me a look of indignation, snorted smoke, and finally relented. Death placed a heaping platter of pancakes on the floor for him. No sooner had I sat on the exceptionally warm seat than Baba Yaga came over for my order.

Yes, that Baba Yaga, the witch from the Slavic folktales who could give blessings or cause menace. If you ask me, that part about blessings was entirely made up.

The old hag hadn't aged a day since she started serving up food at the diner. Of course, she was so marked with warts and wrinkled skin, it was hard to tell. Baba Yaga refused to wear the diner's red and white uniform, saying she didn't look good in those particular colors. Instead she wore a green hoodie, gypsy skirt, and a large brass medallion. Her jewelry was as ugly as she was without filigree or etching of any kind and it made me think of the same one that Mildred wore. She stood there on her chicken feet with her order pad ready, and I waited for her to ask the question that she was famous for.

"Did you come of your own free will or did someone send you?"

Answer wrongly and you didn't get any food. "Free will, Baba. No one ever sends me."

She nodded curtly. "So what will it be?"

I had a hankering for steak and eggs, but Gim's story about the Fukushima Prime put me off. "I'll have what they're having."

"Chocolate chip pancakes," she announced in her burbling voice. "Drink?"

"Coffee."

She nodded before turning her face toward the order window. "Another order of collision mats with dirt, Sal. And a cup of Joe." Baba Yaga glanced at me with rheumy eyes. "Won't be but a few. Don't gnaw on the napkins." When she said it, she looked right at the Hellhound, who innocently licked his chops.

"I'll make sure he only eats a few," Death said.

She harrumphed, absently closing her gnarled fingers around her medallion. "Good luck with that." I could hear her mumble as she toddled away, "Damned dog drools all over the tiles and then they melt." A few minutes later, she returned with my meal, purposely kicking Smokie in the hind parts as she maneuvered around him. Baba Yaga was a piece of work. Shadow Street was the perfect place to keep her out of trouble.

I dug in, thinking how fortunate it was that I had taught the Aztecs how to grow cacao beans.

"Tell him, Beka," Death said between his own mouthfuls.

Beka dabbed at her lips before answering. "I talked to Levi Vrille today."

Vrille was the administrator of the Crazy as a Bed Bug Lunatic Asylum. "What did he have to say?"

"He stumbled across Doc Goodman before he died. He said Doc was still talking, but he had a strange accent."

"What kind of accent?"

"The kind you have when you wake up after being hit in the head."

"Dysprosody?"

"Yeah. I got the lecture on how a cerebrovascular accident causes the right hemiplegia. Anyway, he finally got around to telling me he spoke in a German accent—a heavy German accent. And you know how Goodman felt about Nazis."

"What did he say?"

"He talked about how *she* used District One magic."

District One? That was a place that existed on Earth in the mid 21st Century after Duvalier ousted the United Nations troops during a world takeover. I had friends there—Marshal Ty Merrick and her partner Andy LaRue. Magic didn't exist, according to Ty, but the folks there cobbled together spells and potions from the leftover junk of a destitute society. "Trash magic?" I asked.

Beka shrugged, studying me for a moment. "I didn't think we had any District One residents here. They know just enough to be dangerous, Thomas. Really dangerous."

"As far as I'm aware, and I get the roster every day of new arrivals, District One is a Red-Band. No one is sent here." I slurped on my coffee, hoping for a different direction. "Maybe he had a stroke."

"Vrille didn't think so. He didn't have any other signs, but he died before they could get him to the hospital. Our coroner never made it out before most of these folks were put in the ground."

"I just saw him, and he said they all died of natural causes except the vamp."

"Well, he lied. I was on the other ones. We sent them off to the morgue right away because Wiley was so far into his cups that we couldn't rouse him."

"Anything odd about the other deaths?"

Beka took a delicate bite and chewed, looking thoughtful. "Not that we could tell. They were stone cold when we got to them."

"There were empty shells," Death said. "There was nothing I could do. Their souls were MIA."

"Did you check that gate over in the Old Quarter?" I asked.

"I did. The wards had slipped a bit and it might have been how the Angel got in. The egress wards are a bit dodgy."

I rubbed a forkful of pancake in maple syrup. "Beka, have you had anyone come to you or your people who are worried about their safety?"

"That happens every day. Folks get into tiffs with each other all the time, but these people who came up dead? Not a peep."

"I wonder if we have someone who snuck in from the Antarian Star Reef."

"That's pretty far uptime, Thomas," Death said. "And they've got it good in the future. Although, they would have the technology to break the ward locks if they saw fit. Don't the Guardians send those folks to Faustus where there aren't any gates?"

"Usually, but we have one Deliosian here. Ker at'em."

"Oh, he'll hurt you," Beka said, adding a tinkling laugh. "Might stab you to death with his watchmaker's awl."

Smokie suddenly whined and huffed a bit of fire. We all glanced toward him, realizing his plate was empty, and the charred end of a paper napkin stuck out of his mouth. Beka sighed. "Why couldn't I have a regular dog?"

I'm sure my expression gave away my surprise. "Beka, you live on Shadow Street. This is a regular dog."

One thing that most people don't know is that going back and forth between gates is a no-no if you're a Human or Human-Hybrid. The nature of the gates changes you, and if you try to re-cross through a gate you've already been through, you have a meltdown at a micro-cellular level that will leave you gooey, gross, and dead. The portals do allow exchanges to happen for the Immortals and most find a junction to cross into Earth plane when they need to refresh supplies. I've known a few, though, who have tried to travel through the gates to get some special magical application only available in one of the Nine Dimensions. They've returned and the minute they step through, they end up candidates for the street sweeper.

Levi Vrille was the head of our lunatic asylum and the only psychotherapist on Shadow Street. He was a big man, with blond hair, blue eyes and a passionate hatred of the Nazi death machine—so he maintained. His last name spoke volumes to me. Vrille was a French word that described the deliberately induced, nose-first spinning descent of an airplane. He claimed to be a Jew from Paris, who had narrowly missed a trip to Auschwitz, but the Guardians in their infinite wisdom thought he was dangerous enough to ship off to our little pocket dimension. Unfortunately, I don't get the tear sheets of background info on all our residents, so I only had my suspicious to go on about Vrille being much more than he claimed.

I found him at his office at the Lunatic Asylum. We called it The Crazy As A Bed Bug Loony-Bin, because in this world of crazies, the worst of the worst were stowed out of sight and out of mind. It broke my heart when I came across people so assigned—folks like Joan of Arc and Nikola Tesla— here because they were in communication with Angels and ETs. They weren't crazy. They were just too dangerous with their genius to be allowed to walk freely down this filthy street. The Guardians didn't want holy riots or death rays to mess up the peaceful little prison world they'd created.

Vrille greeted me with a smile and big cup of coffee, which I didn't drink because I didn't trust him not to put some psychedelic drug into it. He sat next to me on his leather couch, wearing a black suit that was too small for him through the shoulders, and languidly smoked a cigarette with a hand-carved bone holder. Had he worn a skull insignia in his lapel, I would have thought him a member of the Nazi SS.

He had an affected French accent, much more so than any Parisian should have. "You are here about poor Dr. Goodwin, no?"

"I was told you were the last to see him alive."

Vrille nodded, and I thought the fabric of his jacket might rip from the movement, but surprisingly it didn't. "Dr. Goodwin had stopped in to my office earlier in the day after checking one of our patients. He didn't look well, and he complained of a migraine. Now, I think it was a prelude to a stroke."

"You found him in an alley outside of the pub?"

"I did. You know I don't drink, but I do take an evening constitutional. I passed said alley and heard someone bark, "*Achtung!*" Well that certainly did get my attention." He paused to puff on the ciggy, and I noticed it was one of those dark chocolate cheroots that are so popular with the French.

"What did you see?"

"Goodwin lying in the alley."

"I know that. Did you see anyone?"

"*Ne*—no."

He almost slipped. I almost had the truth on him for my own satisfaction. "Any signs of violence?"

"No. He merely stated that someone—a female had used District One magic upon him." He puffed again, blowing a smoke ring. "He spoke with a

German accent which tells me he suffered from dysprosody. Combined with his complaints of earlier in the day, I assumed it was a stroke. I called the emergency unit, but he died before they could reach him."

"Did he say anything else?"

"No. He just said, 'she did it'. She did it."

I studied him for a moment. Either this closet Nazi was lying or Goodwin's murder had nothing to do with the others. If his essence had been stolen, death would have been immediate.

"Did you stay with him the entire time while you waited for the ambulance?"

"I did leave him for a few minutes to wait on the paramedics."

"Did anyone enter the alley while you were on the street?"

"I don't know. Perhaps. There were many people about. When I finally returned to him, Dr. Goodwin had passed peacefully into that good night."

"Do you recall anything else? Anybody out of the ordinary?"

Vrille glanced at me and spread his hands wide in a submissive gesture. "Honestly, Mr. Thomas. That is all I know. The medics came and took him away to the coroner, I presume."

I nodded and rose to go. "Who had the good doctor visited?"

"Napoleon," he answered. "You know the Emperor is a Shapeshifter? His lunacy is making it difficult for him to maintain his Humanity. He's phasing, poor fellow. It won't be long before he goes."

"Can I speak with him?"

"*Sacré bleu!* No. He's sedated. He has been shifting into a lion and attacking patients. We can't have that." He paused to puff again, a thoughtful look on his square jawed face. "It is truly evidence of inferior mentality when a person shifts into a beast."

"They all shift into beasts," I said.

Vrille turned to regard me with a matter-of-fact expression. "And so the entire subspecies is inferior. Period."

I nodded, piqued that he spoke of many of my friends in that manner, but I let it go. I was obviously not going to get squat out of him. "Well, if you think of something else, please get in touch with me."

He puffed away, waving a hand at me. "But of course. Always willing to participate in a manhunt."

I left the office and walked out into the quiet hallway, pausing to rehash the conversation. As I stood there, I was approached by a Tink, one of those little Fae who are no bigger than your finger. She landed on the back of my hand and motioned to me. I raised her to my ear and her voice came in a sudden roar that made my eyes water.

"Angel, the Vrille is lying to you. Goodwin was not here."

"Why would he lie about that?"

"Unknown. But I can tell you this. Vrille is seeking a *portae aditu*."

When the Tink said that, I lowered my hand to study her.

She smiled. "Not for him, but to bring in his cohorts."

"Who?"

"This I cannot say out loud. But I'm sure you have divined that for yourself because, well, he doesn't hide it as thoroughly as he believes with that fake French accent." She lifted off my hand and floated near my face. "That and the fact that he's been known to exact experiments on those who cannot speak for themselves. But that is a matter for another day, I suppose."

"How do you know this?"

She laughed and it was the same sound made by the sweet bells on a tinker's wagon. "Because I'm one of the inmates here. I get out of the cage they keep me in. Folks don't usually pay attention to someone the size of a hummingbird."

Here on Shadow Street, magic is real, driven by the consumption of quantum mechanics. Words have power, because they always have. According to the Holy Bible, God spoke the Universe into existence. The ancient Egyptians would divide up words when writing so as to dampen their power. The Druids of old Ireland created spells—special words that held energy enough to levitate the monoliths that created Stonehenge. It's all based on the Angelic secrets of Enochian magic and because it is so powerful, the Guardians made sure that there is a dampening field surrounding Shadow Street. There are zones, though, where the suppression is weak due to atomic flux, and occasionally, folks like Aleister Crowley discover a weak spot and try to create havoc. I recently found him nearly cracking the codes on the gates to invite demons into our world. I had to do a little memory smother on him, something I like to avoid. It's an Angelic lobotomy and not something I'm proud to say that I'm good at. But I am.

Still, for the most part, folks try to use their power for the good of all concerned, even if it mostly falls flat. People can talk themselves into anything when they believe hard enough.

I sat in the third floor flat belonging to Old Herman the Mage, waiting patiently for his widow, Bree, to finish fussing over the tea service. She was as ancient as they come, probably close to two hundred years old, skinny, and wearing a pair of baggy capris that hit her ankles, because she was so short. Her fuzzy hair was dyed orange, and her red lipstick was smeared across one cheek. Like the other crones I'd seen or met with, she too, sported a brass medallion around her neck.

Bree moved with the alacrity of someone thirty years old. After she poured me tea, she didn't sit, but instead struck a yoga pose known as the tree—whereby she stood on one foot while the other rested against her inner thigh.

"I hope you don't mind, Thomas," she trilled. "Yoga helps to calm me."

"Not at all." I took a moment to scan the apartment. It looked like an alchemist's laboratory, complete with liquid-filled beakers, bottles, bowls, hoses—all sitting upon sturdy wooden tables. Charms hung from the ceiling fan, bobbling as the blades turned slowly. There was a collection of bones and a human skull etched with mystical symbols that were rubbed with lampblack. The dining room table, made from oak straight out of the Black Forest, was covered with scrolls, parchment books, two or three wands, a pair of brass knuckles, a couple of knitting needles, a scrying mirror, and a box with several metal doohickies sticking out of it.

"What is that?" I asked, pointing to it.

She glanced toward the box. "That is a dimensional defibrillator."

"What does it do?"

"It breaks through the dimensional barriers so we can contact our children on Earth plane." Bree dropped her foot and came to sit in the overstuffed chair beside the couch. A puff of dust rose when she flopped into it. "We have five kids still on the other side. The Guardians decided they had nothing to do with Herman's activities and so were granted permission to remain Earthside. I had nothing to do with his activities either, in case you are wondering. But, a wife goes where her husband goes."

I had my doubts, but I had to ask. "Does the defibrillator work?"

"Sometimes. When the weather is right and the source energy is vital."

"Source energy?"

"Herman used his own energy, his body's electrical impulse to make it work. He was getting old, so he had to rely on bonding magic to get it done."

I sipped my tea, trying not to look excited at what she was telling me. "What type of bonding magic?"

"You take the blood of a willing host and read a spell over it. It separates the plasma from the cells and charges it with vital forces. You then mix it into an elixir. I used pineapple juice and raspberry in season. Drink it down and it bonds to the DNA, enhancing the source energy."

"Who was his willing host?"

"Me, of course." She squinted. "You don't think my Herman had anything to do with these killings, do you?" Bree paused to blow out a hard breath. "I mean, how could he? He's dead, too."

"I don't think he was involved, Bree, but I'm wondering if there is someone here on Shadow Street who is holding a grudge against him. Herman was using Humans to further his experiments."

"No, he never harmed a Human. He may have exacted revenge upon a few Nazis, but they were animals."

"What about Levi Vrille?"

Bree puffed her cheeks up. "You know he's a Nazi, right? He talks like he's a victim, but he's not. He and Herman hated each other. Herman fought in the German resistance. Took a bullet to the belly for his efforts. He avoided Vrille. They all did."

"Vrille said he found Goodman still alive."

"I doubt that."

"Why?"

"Because Goody knew about his Mengele-like experiments at the loony-bin."

I immediately wished I had some more information on Vrille and his identity, but somehow, his background had been redacted. I was in the dark about him.

"How do you know about them?"

"Because I'm a busy-body and when Herman was out with his friends, I turned the defibrillator onto the neighbors. Vrille lives a couple of blocks over. He's an evil one, so I made it my business to check him out." She shrugged. "Maybe he somehow found out and he killed my Herman because of it."

I moved my questions farther afield. "Did Herman know the other victims outside of the drink-fests at the Gargoyle?"

"Herman rarely talked about them. None ever came by for a visit. I think most people, including his drinking buddies, avoided Herman because he was such a powerful mage."

"What about the vampire?"

Bree frowned. "She was some sort of call girl. Not part of their group as far as I know."

"Did you ever join them?"

"Me? I'm a teetotaler. And I'm a Midnight Witch. We don't imbibe, because it diminishes our powers."

"What genus of Midnight Witch?"

She scowled. "You'll hold it against me for sure, if I tell you."

"Bree, don't make me go around you."

"Well, if you must know, I'm a Fuath."

Fuath. In the old language, she dealt in spells of hate and discord.

"I supposed you can't deny your birthright now can you?" she asked.

It took me a moment to realize that the energy coming off of her was especially dark. My natural Angelic strobe kept me from being affected by the baddies and unless I was open to it, I didn't get a whiff of energy off of anybody. "You're not planning revenge for Herman's murder, are you?"

She shook her head. "We are all responsible for our own destinies. Besides, my powers were never very strong. I wanted to be a homemaker, which always riled my mum. That's why I married, had kids, and devoted my time to Herman's projects. I was a pretty good wife, too. Loved my kids, although I hated their girlfriends and boyfriends. I did my best, though."

I nodded and glanced around. "What alchemical experiment was he working on?"

"Not alchemy. He was seeing if it was possible to contain the Odic fluid."

It was my turn to scowl. "He was seeking to collect the essences of life?"

Bree flounced out of the chair and resumed her yoga asana. "My Herman was that way. I kept telling him it was all bunk, but he was dead set on capturing it."

"Why?"

"Why? He wanted to sell the stuff. His motto? Lose a loved one? We can reanimate them." She dipped forward to regard me with a hawkish expression. "My Herman was demented. I don't know about the others."

Shadow Street is not one long street. Shadow Street is a place, a city of life and death. It has neighborhoods that are urban and decayed, and it has wide-open spaces like Abduction Park where you can walk your dog and get the occasional joyride in a flying saucer. Shadow Street has nymph pools and deep forests, old creepy oaks, things living in the hedgerow, rivers of three-eyed fish that are great eating, and the occasional cave neighborhood with mailboxes lining the path up to the entrances. We also have a manufacturing quarter where cloth is milled, brooms are cut, and bricks are made. We have a power plant for electricity, too. It's a bit dodgy, the turbines held together with magic and bailing wire, but it manages to churn out enough sparkles to run the computers and keep the lights on after a plane shift.

There are some powerful people who live here on Shadow Street, mainly because it keeps them out of the mainstream of the Earth Plane. They have keys to move back and forth through at least two of the gates and any portal they so choose. I have no say about their comings and goings, because at least two of them could squash me like a bug if I dared interfere in their travels. I'm talking about The Sisters—Cinere and Corvus.

There were created at the beginning and for centuries were known as The Fates, those creatures who ruled man's destiny. They've been known by many names in many cultures and at one time there had been three, but the third goddess who had been called Atropos or in modern parlance, the Unturnable, was missing in action. Atropos was apparently a stickler about unalterable destinies and the others wanted more freedom to dick with Humanity. When the dimensions splintered, Cinere and Corvus changed their names from Lachesis, the Allotter, and Clotho, the Spinner, to monikers that meant Ashes and Raven.

Cinere liked the darkness left over from the brightness of fire and would disappear into the Ninth Dimension to make Lumiel's life a heated misery. Corvus occasionally messed with Odin and shifted into one of his birds, Huginn and Muninn—Thought and Memory—delivering to him dirty jokes as well as unhappy endings. In other words, you do not want to mess with The Sisters unless you bring cake with lots of icing.

When I decided to visit them, I brought two kinds of cake. Cinere liked Italian Buttercream and Raven liked Red Velvet. They met me at the door of their steampunk shack and when they saw I was carrying goodies, invited me in for a cup of coffee to go with the cake.

The two were like a billion years old, but their glamour presented two hot chicks—one with red hair and the other with blond. They were beautiful in a lethal kind of way. I was installed in their library which was floor to ceiling books, computers and monitors. A bit unsettling when you got a look at the decayed condition of the rest of the house. We made pleasantries as Cinere cut the sweets, and I took a moment to pet their fat *Fumus*, Adipem, a sentient creature similar to a house cat that could disappear like smoke. She was in a bad mood on this day, because a certain rodent kept eluding her. She said hello and asked after my health, but before I could tell her, she stalked away and vanished with a lingering smell of lilacs while lisping something about 'severely stretching a mousie's neck from his body'.

Even though they were the Fates, they served as unofficial Watchers here on Shadow Street. They maintained the Internet network by interfacing to a character who was trapped dimensionally intestate when the Universe splintered. He called himself the Wizard of Zo, a Geek's geek, who couldn't personally escape his own sphere, but who could transfer packets of information via the celestial information highway between all ten dimensions.

Cinere handed me a slice from each cake on a filthy plate with a crusty spoon. Dirt didn't bother me, but I did have a momentary worry that Adipem had licked the silverware. They both joined me, sitting in ratty wing back chairs, making slurping noises with their coffee and small sounds of orgasm over the dessert.

"I'm sorry to bother you, ladies," I began. "But I need your help."

"We were wondering how long it would be before you stopped by," Cinere said. "Corvus has been waiting for you. She put mascara on two days ago."

"Cinere!" Her sister spit, pieces of cake flying out behind her words.

Corvus had a crush on me, and I really didn't mind. It was always good to have a Fate like the shape of your butt. I smiled at her and then gave her one of those, we'll-talk-later winks.

She smiled alluringly and then took a huge bite of cake.

"What do you need, Thomas?" Cinere asked. "Would you like to know about the dead Angel?"

"Exactly. Who was he?"

Corvus spoke up. "He was a Neph, not a full blown Angel like you. His mama was a woman named Eliza Blackthorne and his daddy was apparently, though this hasn't been confirmed, Archangel Raphael. We haven't been able to get him on the horn to verify."

"You wouldn't. Raph hates modern technology." I took a bite of cake and got a bit of crunchy dirt with it. "I was told this Neph was going around telling folks he was here to take my job. True?"

Cinere cackled, a rather unusual sound coming out of a beautiful mouth. "Like a Neph could take over governership for an Enochian Angel. Impossible."

"He brought something with him," Corvus said. "His bluster was just stupidity."

"What did he bring?"

Corvus glanced at Cinere, and I knew there was a destiny event tied up with the answer. It made me tingle in all the wrong places.

"Please, ladies," I whispered. "I need to know."

Corvus nodded. "Yes, you do, and I'm sorry about this."

Cinere loosed the bomb. "He brought over a copy of the *Enacteron*."

I almost dropped my cake. The *Enacteron* was the Book of Days Grimoire that held the Magic of Eternity. It was stored in the Hall of Akashic Records to make it difficult to access. I knew the *Enacteron* backwards and forwards because I had written all the spells contained within it.

The Hall, where it had supposedly been protected, was located in a spiral plane wedged between the Earth and the Nine Dimensions. The spiral was different than our little time slip. Here, things could change. There, time spiraled in on itself to the point that it didn't really exist. One or two Guardians had the ability to access the Hall and these gals could make the leap, but a Neph? He was only half Angel, even though that part of him was descended from the Enochian class. His Human side would have made it impossible for him to bring out the book. He had to have had help.

Corvus knew what my next question was, but before I could ask it, she raised a finger, and placed her plate on a wobbly wooden table. She slipped over to one of the computer terminals and dialed up Audia, an instant message program we used on Shadow Street. Seconds later, I saw the screen morph, and there was Zo's smiling face staring at us. He looked like a fresh-faced kid, but he was as ancient as they came.

"Hey, Tommy," he greeted, knowing how I hated the nickname. "What's shakin'?"

"The usual, Zo. What do you have for me?"

He glanced off to his right before returning his attention to me. "The *Enacteron*. Sorry to say, but that was the last physical copy left in the Hall. Since everything went electronic, only those with creds can access the password system to the Akashic database. But, the Library is still open for Immortals. Getting that book past the door took some power." He typed on his keyboard and then said, "The Neph didn't access the Hall, of course. The system would have scorched him to ashes."

Cinere giggled, and Zo grinned.

Suddenly, my patience evaporated like a *Fumus*. "Who took the book of spells, Zo?" I asked sharply.

"Well, I can't be sure, but the last name on the sign out card says it was Archangel Michael."

Shadow Street looks like a gloomy Cuba. Our transportation is stuck in the 1950s, which is okay, because our roads are pretty much straight out of the 1930s. Plus, people like to do it themselves here, and we manufacture our own parts over in the factory district. The cars, the Old Yellow Cabs salvaged from a bygone era of Earth, the trollies, and the trucks all meet our needs since many of our residents prefer to hoof it, wing it, or shift into something with four legs for added speed. I will, on occasion, take a cab, but for the most part, the potholes in the roads are so bad, it practically gives my spleen a massage and I'm not up for that too often.

It was quiet when I stepped out onto the street. Even during festival time, when dinnertime came around, the traffic would slow to a trickle. Most folks would rush home to feed their families and prepare to listen to the broadcasted game between the Woodhogs and the Goatmen. There were a few drunks spilling out of the Gargoyle, but even they seemed subdued, and I wondered if it were because of the news about the deaths. The editor-in-chief of the Shadow Street Gazette, Sally Freeman, had run some speculative articles about the lingering murder-death mystery. She had been a journalist of some repute until she'd gotten on the wrong side of

William Randolph Hearst and found herself without a job and without a desk Earthside. We had an agreement, she and I. Sally could print what she felt important, but if she found out any secrets, like the locations of backdoor portals, she could not spread the word or even allude to the fact.

Yes, it is censorship. So, sue me. Shadow Street isn't the USA.

I'd walked about twenty feet and paused, my thoughts chewing on this new information. What was Michael doing checking out the book? Was he trying to find the ultimate secret, the one I carried around in my noggin? If so, he wouldn't find it in the Grimoire. That was mostly a book of high level spells—summonings, sendings, maskings. It had been centuries since I glanced at the book, but I couldn't recall anything that would steal a person's essence, unless someone had revised the text.

I pulled out my cellphone and using the network shunted through Zo's dimension, tried to place a call to Michael. He didn't answer, and if he had, I figured he would have sidestepped my question. I left a voicemail, not expecting much.

My concern veiled my usual vigilance. That's when the attack came. Something unseen grabbed me from behind. It was strong, so strong that it flung me like a rag doll into the alley next to Puck's Pickle Palace where I landed on a heap of slimy garbage overflowing from the dumpster. In the dim light, I could barely detect a glimmering streak of sparkles and then it punched me hard in the chin, followed by a right cuff to the side of my head. It then grabbed my forearm and delivered a burn straight into my skin.

Well, that just pissed me off. I may look like an everyday angel, but I'm not. When I say I'm an Enochian Angel, I mean I'm one of the old ones, and when I want to use my inherent power, woe to the person who comes up against me. I unfurled the full size of my wings, using them for leverage.

Another vicious assault came at me, delivered as punches to my stomach. I still couldn't see anything, but I didn't need to.

It's like a fireball in my solar plexus, a point of pure zero point energy that was gifted to the original Angels. If I brought the full power to bear, I could kill this invisible entity, but I could also either trap it, transform it, or wink it out of existence, depending upon my mood—and right now, my mood was angry. Using my wings, I found my balance and with a small flap of feathers, I rose above the commotion and the battering to my mid-section. I hovered there, trying to see what creature assaulted me. It poked at my calves, stinging hits that felt like knives.

Enough. I called the fire into my hands and with a swooshing maneuver; I delivered it fore, aft, starboard, and port. An Angelic wind abruptly washed through the alley, blowing trash and rats caught in the stream and delivering them into a swirling vortex that formed before me. The sparkle suddenly wavered, turned an orange-green, and then upon the roar of the wind, I heard a prolonged screech. Low, keening, and female.

Something made me hesitate—call it my soft spot for living creatures. I lowered the intensity of my onslaught, releasing my attacker, who just as quickly as it had come, was gone.

When an angel calls on that kind of energy, it signals others to his or her plight. Of course, Archangel Michael arrived after the final blow, and if you ask me, it was perfectly timed. He showed up in all his Pearlescent glory right there, glowing white wings extended so far the tips touched the buildings on either side of the pickle alley. He could make bleach blonds swoon in hair envy with his long, flowing platinum locks. Michael was playing the savior it seemed, visiting while wearing his golden armor and most beautiful countenance. His visit annoyed me more than the attack.

He held out his hand to help me up. "What is the loathsome smell?" he asked.

I stood, wiped at crud on the butt of my jeans and sighed. "That, Brother, is what's left over from a kimchi pot. And now I have it on me."

Michael studied me for a moment. "Are you all right?"

Okay, I'd had enough. "What do you care? You plunk me in the middle of this world for no other reason than me using my brains to escape Pompeii the day Mount Vesuvius erupted."

"It was because of your brains, we assigned you here. Who better than to watch a world full of genius-level miscreants than the king of them all?"

It was my turn to study him. "Jealous?"

We stepped back out onto the lonely street before he answered me. "I'm not jealous, but there are those Guardians who are. They follow the rules, and they don't like it when an upstart Slate gives away their secrets to Humans."

"Oh, you mean teaching the poor creatures how to read, write, and think for themselves? The Guardians diddled with their genes and when they couldn't wipe them off the Earth with flood and famine, they blame me for trying to sort out a decent solution for both sides. The Humans gave them their due in worship and sacrifices. I think they got their money back."

Michael shrugged. "What you did was give us a planet full of drunks when you taught them to make wine and beer."

"Oh boo-hoo, cry me a river. They needed to stay drunk with people like Ares and Thor running around loose." I paused to wipe a piece of cabbage off my face. "I want to know about this rogue Neph you sent here."

He scowled, and that beautiful countenance faltered. I could see the ugliness it hid. "I sent no Neph here."

"He was disguised as a Pearl. Had wings and lovely toenail polish."

"I had no part of it." Michael glanced toward a dark corner of the alley and that told me everything I needed to know.

"Well, he's not going to be a problem anymore."

"Why?"

"Squashed like a bug. Someone stole his essence."

Michael lifted his chin to study me. "Why would someone do that?"

I had my ideas, but I wasn't about to give them away to the avenging Angel so he could swoop in and take the killer out of my hands. Glancing down, I noticed my forearm had been raked right across my ouroboros tattoo. This was the *portae aditu*, the key that locked and unlocked the gates. "Tell me, Michael, are the Guardians granting new *portae aditu*?"

"No, we are not."

It was my turn to get into his face. "You're lying."

I saw him blink back a bit of murderous rage, but then he tried to change the subject. "Well, anyone could have the tattoo, but it doesn't do a bit of good without…" He stopped speaking to stare at me. "Without the proper essence."

Michael growled a bit and disappeared.

I stood there, taking a moment to collect myself and scrape away bits of chopped ginger that were starting to burn the cuts on my arm. As I did, one of those Elementals swirled silently into the alley. Fog.

Nature Elementals speak in pictures more than words, but Fog was an ancient construct and had learned long ago how to whisper in a rudimentary language I could understand. He greeted me and said, "White Angel dangerous. Give book to Neph. Fog see."

I went home, took a shower, and then another one. The briny smell of kimchi stuck to my feathers, leaving me a bit nauseous. I sprinkled on some Old Woods Spicy, cologne made by Teresa Acar, a Wood Rose Elf with a great nose for scents and a talent for decanting them as fragrances. Old Woods Spicy seemed to work, but the spell attached to the scent made my lips tingle.

I needed to sleep. Calling up the zero-point energy was exhausting. So, I lay down, intending to take a quick nap. I awoke eight hours later with a stiff jaw, a pounding headache, and worried someone else had gotten murdered while I dreamed of Heaven.

Stepping out again, I realized that the clock had swung to the High Day of Ritual that happened two days before Moon Kiss. Shadow Street was abuzz with life. Vendor stalls had sprung up at the Marketplace, street corner altars were crammed with fresh flowers and leis, and there were queues out the doors for many of the local businesses. The smells of roasting meat and baking bread nearly undid me. People shopped for the noonday meal, made absolutions, some stretched into their natural forms, and most of the residents greeted me with hardy handshakes as well as free snacks. I walked toward my destination, chomping on a piece of cheesecake and slurping a sugary pop that tasted like it was made from the char left on the bottom of a rice cooker.

My next stop was to see Dr. Goodman's widow, Mariah. I came to their clinic and saw it was jammed with patients. A harried nurse greeted me and proceeded to put me into an examining room where I read the wall charts relating to the internal issues of several different species. I was just reading about the eye troubles of Wolpertingers when Mrs. Goodman dropped in.

Mrs. Goodman was a Bast—part Cat, part Human—and all gorgeous. She had the almond shaped eyes and small chin of a feline. Her body was lithe. I could almost see her muscles rippling beneath her skin. She had delicate rosettes on her honey-colored skin and a tail—a beautiful tail that flicked to show her annoyance at my inopportune appearance. Despite this, she did her best to smile, displaying tiny fangs and perfect white teeth.

"I was wondering when you might stop by," she said. "I just didn't expect it on the busiest day of the week."

I smiled. "Sorry. The investigation has taken me longer than I thought."

She glanced at my boogered arm and ran a finger across it. "I have just the salve that will close up that wound. It looks like you were clawed." Mariah opened a nearby cabinet and pulled forth a jar of white cream. She gently applied it. "My husband always thought my herbals worked wonders," she whispered. "Even on Immortals who are supposed to be able to heal immediately."

"Yeah, well, I don't know any Immortals that can do that. We might not die from the wounds, but it does take us a bit to heal." I watched her ministrations for a moment before launching into the interview. "Was Charles ill before he died?"

"Ill? Goody may have been old, but he was as strong as a horse."

"No problems with hypertension?"

She paused in applying her magical salve to study me. She had eyes the color of old bronze, and I thought for the thousandth time about what she could have seen in that old fart she had married. "You've talked to Levi Vrille. He's full of crap, you know. He didn't have a stroke and he didn't have dysprosody. I don't know what Vrille was getting on about. I don't even believe he found Goody alive." Her tail swished harder the longer she spoke.

"Vrille seemed surprised he was speaking German giving Charles' hatred of the Nazis."

Mariah snorted delicately. "Really? Well, I supposed Vrille didn't know much about Goody, despite his desire to be one of the group that gathered to drink at the Gargoyle."

"Why do you say that? Didn't Charles hate the Nazis and fight in World War II?"

"Of course, he did. But Goody was from Berlin. German was his first language."

"Who was the last patient Charles saw before he died?"

She shook her head. "Hang on." Turning, she flung open the exam room door and called down the hall to the nurse. "Eppie, bring in the patient logs from the day Goody died."

A moment later, I heard the determined footsteps of the nurse pounding down the hallway. She came in, handed the folder to Mariah, and left without even glancing my way. Mariah shuffled through the sheets. "He saw Baba Yaga just before he left for the Gargoyle."

"What did she see him for?"

"A throat infection."

A throat infection. Now wasn't that interesting?

"Did he know what caused it?"

"He thought it was the jewelry she wore."

"A big golden medallion?"

"Yes, but it wasn't gold. It was something else and it affected her auric field. She refused to take it off. You know how stubborn she can be." Mariah finished with the salve and absently screwed the lid back on. "Personally, I think her throat was infected from all that screeching and keening she does."

We have an alien abduction problem on Shadow Street. An evening walk in Abduction Park will usually net you a ride on a saucer, bag you a computerized implant up your nose, or give you the sky willies for the rest of your life. They use their future technology to slide through the dimensions and scoot through the gates, leaving no imprint and not setting off the alarms. When you approach them, they will register whether you are mortal or immortal. If you are the latter, they scatter like a pack of *Fumi*— smoke and mirrors—leaving behind nothing more than fingernail clippings and the occasional black eyeball.

The Guardians of Eternity consider them the harbingers of Ragnorok. They refuse to speak or write about them because it suggests that there is no eternity and immortality is nothing more than hardy DNA with telomeres that replicate much better than the average mortal. The existence of these extraterrestrial creatures suggests that there is more than our understanding and more to the Unknowable Cosmic Consciousness. It even gives Zeus a headache when he thinks about it.

I left the doctor's office and headed over to our new goldsmith, the Delosian, Ker At'em.

The Delosian Faction aren't really Humans or Supernaturals. They are ETs that got caught up in the great dimensional splinterthon, just like several other alien species. They aren't the time hopping, end-times marauders, and if caught with their pants down in the park when the gray guys zoom in, Delosians will run away screaming like the rest of us. No one likes the anal probe.

Ker At'em was a rogue scientist who literally caused a world of hurt on Delos, so he was shipped here, and stripped of his ability to get the needed supplies to make massive mischief. Massive mischief, maybe not, but mischief on a smaller scale, most definitely.

I walked into his jewelry shop, the tinkling bell above the door announcing my arrival. Ker At'em hadn't been on Shadow Street long, but he'd already stocked his store with bobbles and bling. The counter held a variety of watches, rings, bracelets, and necklaces. He glanced up at my entry, the jeweler's loop covering his cyclopean eyeball that sat in the middle of his pointed head. Flinging it away, he stood, a little orange man with a large mouth, spindly arms, and three fingers on each hand. He had no hair—on his head—but he did have a shaggy unibrow the color of charcoal.

He brought his hands together in a prayer, bowing slightly. "I am honored by your visit, Sir Angel."

I usually hate all the misters and sirs and just want folks to call me Thomas, but this time, I figured I better demand respect. "We have a problem," I began in my ancient Angel baritone voice, "and you're at the heart of it."

He dropped his hands and his unibrow turned into a u-shape. "I have done nothing. I am simply trying to earn a living."

I glanced into his jewelry case. There, nestled on a bed of black velvet was a brass medallion. I pointed to it. "That, I believe, is the problem."

Ker at'em frowned, his unibrow dipping the other direction. He pulled it out of its glass locker. "I don't see how."

I took it from him and the moment I touched it, I felt the power. I fumbled to flip it open. It appeared empty, but there was obviously some sort of power source imbedded in the metal. "This isn't brass, is it?"

"It's filium. Some from my home world."

"What does it do?"

He blinked at me. "Nothing harmful. It is a container for black-body radiation."

"Thermal radiation?"

"Yes. It contains a continuous frequency spectrum that depends upon the body's temperature. The spectrum peaks at a certain frequency and then shifts to higher frequencies when the temperature is achieved. It makes a person feel lively and happy."

I stared at him and then at the object in my hand. "It shifts energy. Does it store energy?"

"Well, yes. That's how it works."

"How hot does it have to get to shift frequencies?"

"I have these set at 80 degrees Fahrenheit. It will grab energy from any heat source and store it."

"How is it released?"

He pulled the medallion from my hand and turned it over. There were two small circular indentations. "You press the lower one and then place it against your heart to release the energy. To store energy, you press the upper one."

"Will it rip off a person's essence?"

Ker At'em stared at me and started to back away, but his jeweler's bench stopped his retreat. I reached over the case and grabbed him by the collar. "Black-body radiation. You jiggered the principle of detailed balance. Didn't you?"

"A person's essence is as hot as a sun. I thought you needed it for a specific reason and mine was not to question her."

"You thought *I* needed it?"

"She said you sent her to buy the four medallions."

My stomach turned. "Who?"

He gulped before answering. "Your female. Esa."

Nephs are the Nephilims of old. They are the ones the Holy Bible says were giants—part Angel, part Man, all bad. Enochian Angels are a priggish lot and since so many of us sit at the council table of the Guardians, we felt we deserved to mate with the daughters of Man. We were comely of face and so were they, which meant, we'd have beautiful, spoiled kids. Turns out, most Nephs were a dirty, rotten lot, who were ugly, callous, and just plain mean. They had to be dealt with for the good of all concerned, so after that water fiasco with Noah, we were a little more careful about spreading around our seed. We manipulated DNA, so a post-flood Neph was an average-sized person who could slide under the Guardians' radar. They had education and jobs and if any Immortal looked at them sideways, he would see nothing more than a regular person. We also did them a disservice for which Nephs never forgave us. Like the offspring of a donkey and a horse, Nephs were the Angelic equivalent of mules. They could never reproduce.

Neph. When Fog had spoken of it, I thought he'd meant Michael had given our dead Neph the book, but he spoke of my Neph. My Esa. The female I'd taken up with for several years, the one who stole my heart and apparently was ready to stomp on it.

I will admit that I've always been an emotional creature. My fellow Angels try to keep their feelings neutral, because they think indulging in laughter or tears is to be too Human and heaven forbid they should emulate beings who they feel are inferior. I never followed suit. I always thought that the ability to feel was a gift of the Creator, and I was always going to use this gift. Still, standing in front of Esa's shop, Halo Tattoo, I wished to hell that I could erase the pain of betrayal that I now experienced.

Halo Tattoo was a shack situated in the Gnarled Oak District. It looked like it was ready to collapse from the outside, but once you entered through the crusty red door, it was a different place. The inside walls and ceilings were made from walnut wood and trimmed in teak. One side of the shop walls sported pages of flash, the basic designs that all tattoo shops offer. The other side was a space for two inking stations, outfitted to the hilt with shelves of supplies, adjustable chairs, and a sound system that pumped out '60s rock. Esa had carved out a homey space for a place where tattoo machines whirred, blood pooled, and people could be brought to tears after hours of being punched with needles.

I opened the door and stomped inside the shop, hoping I'd affected an indignant stride. Her assistant, Zeke, leaned over a client who sweated at the sting of the needle. Zeke glanced up and the scowl I saw on his face told me everything I needed to know. The Halo Tattoo now belonged to him.

"Where is she?" I roared.

The guy sitting in his chair jumped, and Zeke dropped the tattoo machine.

"I said, where is she?"

"It's not my f-fault, Thomas," Zeke said.

"I don't care whose fault it is. Where is she?"

"Chimera Gate. If you hurry, you can catch her."

Crap. The gate with the bad wards. Now I knew why. She was in league with the three bubble, bubble, toil and trouble witches. They needed to kill innocents to marshal up the steam to break the wards and they'd been doing it in degrees, slowly, carefully, hoping no one would notice or figure out the plan until it was too late. I'd never even suspected. Without a doubt, my smart, beautiful Esa had been behind it. She'd found a way to smash the locks and escape—to leave Shadow Street—and me.

Then, I realized something else. She had the Grimoire and I knew what spell she intended to use. It wouldn't work, not on her. Not on a Neph.

I charged from the shop and spread my wings. Flying would be faster than running. As I rushed to the Chimera, my thoughts clicked into clarity. Esa had a new tattoo on her hand—the Ourbouros. When I asked her about it, she said she had admired the one on my arm and since we were a couple, she wanted one, too. Stupid, naive me. I thought she was being serious. The design was the *portae aditu*—the keys that opened the gates— but you needed the proper essence to cook the lock. Esa had been gently and quietly stealing my energy—probably while I slept. No wonder I felt like death warmed over after our little vacation. When it wasn't enough, she went in league with the witches—Baba Yaga, Mildred, and Bree. They had enough power to collect the rest of the essences and to give each a dollop for escape.

I arrived just as Esa and the trouble sisters were pulling down the gate's wards. The Chimera was a gate hidden down a dark swath of an alley in the seedy neighborhood called Bodmin Skull between Nick's Potions and Arlene's Dress Shop. It was in a dark neighborhood where Midnight Witches and Moon Fae lived. The Chimera was an alternate *portae aditu*, a secret doorway that led first to Lumiel's home turf in the Ninth Dimension. Esa was a Nephilim with rare time travel abilities, and she must have thought she could bugger her way past the Infernal guards to access the Earth plane. She couldn't.

She stared at me as I landed several yards from her. Blond, beautiful, and despite her angelic age, she looked like she was just old enough for a good romp in the hay. Esa slowly pointed a sawed off double-barrel shotgun my way. It stopped me in my tracks, more from disbelief than from fear.

"Esa, what are you doing?" I asked, my voice cracking with barely suppressed emotion.

"I'm leaving, Thomas," she answered flatly. "I don't belong here. I helped you escape Pompeii and for that, the Guardians punished me by putting me in this prison. I've bided my time while trying to figure out my escape and when the Delosian came to town, I saw my chance and I'm taking it."

"If you walk through that gate, you'll be trapped in a true hell. The gate is called Chimera for a reason. It splits your DNA, and divides your cells and washes out the differences. Your witch friends will lose their supernatural base and become Human. You'll become Human."

Esa raised her chin. "Or, they'll lose their Human qualities and become all supernatural and I'll become all Angelic. I have worked the spell to create the situation."

"The spell in the Grimoire won't work. It was placed in there as a temporary masking for the Angels during the time of the Dissolution."

She shook her head. "You may have written the book, Thomas, but my father helped me divine the proper code to apply it."

"Raphael?"

"No, you idiot. My father is Michael."

Holy Cats. He was one of the meanest Angels that ever tread on Earth. He wasn't Commander of the Heavenly Host for nothing. "You blackmailed him, didn't you?"

"Let's just say I know a few things that the Guardians would like to know, specifically about how many Nephs are Michael's issue."

"So, he sent your half-brother with the book. And then you killed him."

Baba Yaga spoke up. "No, you stupid featherbrain. I killed him."

53

I ignored her, which I'm sure pissed off the old biddy.

"Listen, Esa, he lied to you. Michael wants you gone and if you step through that gate, you'll become Lumiel's problem."

"I'm leaving, Thomas."

Defeat raged through me. What was I going to do? "So what we had was all a game to you?"

She shook her head sadly. "No, never a game. I love you, Thomas, but I can't spend eternity in this cesspit called Shadow Street. You might consider it home, but I belong out there, where I can time trip. It's part of my inherent nature. I'll lose my mind if I'm forced to deny that part of myself much longer."

I pointed to the three witches. Baba Yaga glared at me while Mildred and Bree made final touches on the wards. The gate rippled and glowed and a glance through it showed a rabbit hole of bright colors. "What about them? They deserve to be here."

"I should have killed you in that alley when I had the chance," Baba Yaga screeched. "I would have had I not slipped on that damned kimchi garbage."

I continued to ignore her by staring at Esa. "That one definitely belongs here." I took a step forward, and as I did, I saw Esa pump the shotgun.

"Stay where you are, Thomas. I've got double barrels loaded with star shot and I will shoot you."

Star shot. The only thing that could smatter an Angel all to hell before he could say 'What happened?'

"You wouldn't," I said. "I must mean more to you than that."

She shook her head. "Compared to my freedom? You don't." Esa glanced quickly at the witches. "Are you done?"

Bree turned toward her. "Yes."

Esa held out her medallion and the witches each touched it with her own. Once done, they waited patiently by the gate. "Don't try to stop us, Thomas. It will end badly for you if you do." She turned toward the witches. "Go."

That was all the encouragement they needed. One by one, they entered the gate, disappearing in a shimmer. Baba Yaga was the last to go, and she paused to flip me the bird. I took an involuntary step forward and when I did, I knew I'd made a serious mistake.

I heard the shotgun blast and felt the slam, hard enough to knock me to the side. As I hit the ground, I briefly wondered what it would be like to finally ascend. I lay there, looking at Esa from an odd angle. She shook her head slowly and stepped through the gate, gone to time and space.

It took me a moment more to realize I wasn't floating in black nothingness. I wasn't dead. I twisted my head to see if half my side was blown away from the star shot, but instead I was met by a face with blue eyes, sharp teeth, and steaming drool. Beka's Hellhound had saved my Angelic life.

Beka and Death had come by to check the wards on the gate. Lucky for me. They accompanied me back to my flat whereby Smokie ripped through the rooms. He chewed on everything, set my duvet on fire, and chased a mouse. He didn't stop when the mouse escaped into a hole in the wall. He rushed against the sheetrock to split it down to the studs.

I honestly didn't have the energy or desire to yell after him. He'd risked his life to push me clear of Esa's murderous attempt and for that, I would always be grateful. Duvets, I could buy. Life, even for an Angel, was a thing that was infinitely precious.

When they were sure I wasn't going to commit Angelic harakiri, Death and Beka left, telling me to meet them at the diner later that evening. I told them I would, but first I had something to do. I changed my clothes, singed on the edges from Smokie's help. I then hit the street, disappearing into the crowds ratcheting up for the first festival of the season.

I took my time, trying to see the world as it was. Shadow Street was not a bad hometown. The people were, for the most part, just trying to get along without too many complications. Life was good here. It suited me. I was just sorry that Esa had not found solace in this plane safe from Lumiel's evil. I tried not to think of her trapped in his most vile of dimensions, but truth be told, it weighed heavy on my mind.

I walked to her small loft apartment. It was quiet and dark inside, the smell of stale coffee perfuming the air.

"Nicki?" I called gently. "Nicki, honey. It's Thomas."

Glancing around, I saw a little smoke and then a black and tan *Fumus* materialized by my feet. She looked at me with sad, green eyes. "She's gone, isn't she?" she lisped. "And she's not coming back."

I squatted down and rubbed her head, marveling at how beautiful this creature was. She was a true Chimera with her fur separated straight down her nose—one side tan, one side black.

"What will I do?" she asked.

"You will come home with me and be my companion," I said. "If that meets with your approval."

If a *Fumus* could smile, Nicki did. She placed a paw on my knee, and I picked her up. I turned to go, but she stopped me.

"You don't serve that fancy schmancy canned *Fumus* food, do you?"

"I don't have to."

"Good," she said, snuggling against my chest. "I much prefer a lovely broiled three-eyed trout for dinner."

Part II

How We Got Here (Well, Kind of)

DEATH BEFORE DRINKING GOAT'S BLOOD
The Cemetery
by Morgan Ashe

I stood outside the mausoleum hidden by the shadows of the scraggly trees that were clumped together to one side of the stone walls. The Dusky Moon didn't add a lot of light to the area, but I didn't need it. Most of the people that lived in Shadow Street had developed superior night vision, and I was no exception. Time had not been kind to this portion of the Shadow Street cemetery. Most of the gravestones leaned, broken and chipped, with moss hiding the names and dates of those buried there. This was the oldest section and some of the gravesites held secrets from centuries long past.

The mausoleum's walls were cracked like the shell of a hard-boiled egg and parts of the wall were pushed outward as if something inside had been trying to crash a way out. The bars on the door and small windows were only there for show. Maybe. The name above the stone-filled door was Pasiphae. I wasn't sure if any of them still lived in Shadow Street, but from the state of decay on the tomb and the graves nearby, I doubted it. The latest date on one of the headstones was a century ago and belonged to a Heli Pasiphae.

I turned my attention back to the larger structure and its cracked walls. One had to have a special kind of Sight or knowledge to see the only thing keeping the monster inside were the various sigils and rune that I knew lined every wall, every opening. Still, the way the walls were pushed out worried me, and I could hear muffled thuds. The entity was not only alive and active but very strong as well. How had it gained that strength when it had been sealed all these years? "Maybe I should have brought backup," I said.

The hairs on the back of my neck suddenly tingled and stood up. Something, no someone, was here with me. Behind me. I could sense a presence, but it wasn't evil. It was like nothing I had ever felt before. The night sounds went still and even the chirp of the insects stopped abruptly. The fresh scent of ozone tickled my nose. I whirled and was face to chest with someone in a dark t-shirt and jeans. He—it was hard to miss the person was a he—grabbed me to keep me from falling backward with hands that were strangely gentle. Where his fingers touched me, hissing blue light arced and crackled. He let go quickly and took a step away from me.

I couldn't see his features hidden by the shadows, but oddly I wasn't afraid. Rather I was intrigued. But still, first things first. "Ouch," I snapped, more for form than actual injury. "Who are you and what did you just do to me? Better yet, why are you here? This is my assignment. Jackson never said anything about backup. I can't believe he'd take a chance and hinder me."

"If you would take a breath, and let me get a word in edgewise, maybe I can answer a few of those questions?" the man said in a deep voice.

A deep voice that does silly things to the inside of my stomach. "Sure, start with the who are you and why are you here, please." Inside I was furiously stifling the *click* that had occurred in my brain the moment he had spoken.

He moved toward me a little but stopped as I stepped back. "Hey, I'm on your side," he said raising his hands. "I had a little personal business and saw you standing here and thought I would come pay a visit. Why are you interested with what's inside?

"Because we are the ones that check on it to make sure it stays in there. No one thought it was awake. Not that anyone really knows what *it* is anymore. My job is to make sure the wards were secure. They aren't. So now I have a different mess to deal with. What was your personal business? This is an odd place to have personal business at 1 a.m." I looked at him suspiciously, wondering if he had been robbing a grave or something worse, but his jeans seemed clean and free of dirt.

"Nosey little thing, aren't you?" His words should have been sarcastic, but the smile on his lips belied that. "I'll tell you after we take care of the little issue in the crypt. How about that?"

"Just tell me. Does it involve grave robbing or anything illegal?"

"Define illegal."

I sighed. "Nevermind. I'll deal with you after this. The thuds are getting louder. Whatever is in there is getting more determined—and violent. I might need to call in reinforcements." I didn't know why I trusted him but something inside of me did.

He walked closer to the structure tilting his head back to look at the stones at the top of the roof. Beams of soft moonlight struck his face and for the first time, his features were revealed to me. A high aquiline nose rose above lips that were just begging to be kissed. Kissed? I shook my head. *That came out of left field. You're here to do a job, not stand and gawk like a schoolgirl at Mr. GQ.*

"Well the wards are there, but the issue is if they will hold. They were put there to keep things from going in, not to keep things from coming out.

They had to have known it would eventually wake. Silly people should know better. Sloppy work if you want my opinion."

"Who are you? Why do you want to help? I don't even know your name."

He turned to face me and stared into my eyes. "My name," he said in an even tone, "is Death. I'm pleased to meet you, Beka."

My heart dropped like a penny in a wishing well. It could only mean one thing. "How do you know my name? OhmyGod. So this is it? My time is up? I'm going to kick the bucket? Meet my maker? Buy the farm? Shuffle—"

"Did you swallow an idiom dictionary? Hush, woman." Death interrupted my feeble attempt to joke about the biggest event in my life...err, death. "I didn't say I was here for you. Like I said it's a bit of personal business. However, if you'd like me to..." His voice trailed off, and he quirked one eyebrow—have I mentioned his perfect eyebrows?—at me.

"No. No, I'm fine. Thanks for the offer though." *Down, girl. You have work to do here and drooling over someone that you suspect worked as one of the Grim Reapers didn't seem like a match made in heaven.*

He was still talking, but I hadn't heard anything he said. I was too busy looking at his lips. They...well, you know – they were perfectly shaped for kissing. "Um, what did you say?" I asked, my attention now fully focused on his words.

He sighed. "I asked you how you plan on keeping that thing from getting loose?"

"Plan?" I asked stupidly. "I was just here to check the wards. I'm not ready to do anything more than that right now." I stuck my hands in my pockets. Salt and some round hard things that I suspected might be coins I had put in the wrong pocket. I could feel the cold blade of my iron knife pressing against my ankle. "Salt and iron."

"Obviously you were never an Angel Scout," he said with a grin. "Lucky for us, I came prepared."

"Hey, now wait a minute. First of all, I was a Cherub so that should account for something. Second of all, I have other skills that may not be readily apparent. I should be able to put runic chains around it and keep it locked up until something permanent can be arranged, depending on what it is. As a last resort, I can send it back to where it came from. I'm not sure that's a good idea unless I know where it came from."

"What in the Nine Gates is a Cherub...nevermind. That's a conversation we can have later over blueberry pancakes. So look inside and tell me what you can see. We need to understand what it is we are dealing with first. I'm not getting a read on anything except sheer hatred."

I turned to the mausoleum and opened my Sight. Immediately, layers upon layers of runes and sigils came into view. Some of the layers were different than others, their energy put down by witches and mages at a later time, possibly in an attempt to further keep the entity imprisoned. I looked at the ground and not only had it been salted, but a large pentagram had been cast into the concrete. Its points came out from each side with the crypt's square foundation resting directly in the center. An inner circle inside the pentagram was also carved with a variety of runes, sigils, and a few other signs that I did not know. *Whoever would use a pentagram when trying to keep something in check? That was definitely sloppy work.*

When I'm using my Sight, it's as if I am viewing two worlds. Reality fades to a gray transparent world and everything my Sight sees is in living color. Ghosts, hidden objects, phantasms, magically laid lines all come into view. What really creeps me out about my Sight, though, is the knowledge that all of this existed in my real world and were there regardless of whether I could see them or not.

I pushed my Sight further. Into the cracks and crevices of the stone walls and into the inner chamber. A metal coffin that had been in there was torn apart, shredded like a cardboard shoebox. Heavy chains were broken and littered the floor. There in the center was a table, its top discolored and stained. *No*, I realized. *An altar.* Then, movement. I saw it. The creature. As my mind tried to understand just what it was, it went abruptly still, its head lifted and a heavy snout sniffed the air, trying to find what it too now sensed. With a cry, I shut down my Sight, but it was too late. Those red, glowing eyes had looked straight at me. I felt its hatred and lust for blood all the way to my soul.

I staggered backwards and almost fell, but Death's hands grabbed my shoulders and steadied me. Again, the blue lightning sparked where we touched for a moment, but then quieted down and stopped. "I'm okay," I said, and then regretted my words when he removed his hands. *Sure, the monster is beating at its cage and you're upset this man you just met isn't touching you. Get a grip, Beka.*

"What did you see?" Death asked, concern apparent in his voice.

I shuddered in remembrance. "A minotaur." I managed to say it without stuttering. I felt foolishly proud of myself for a moment and then surrendered to the inevitable and hugged myself for comfort. "A minotaur."

"That's minotaur with a capital 'M'," Death said and pecked me on the nose. *How did he know?*

"Isn't he supposed to be guarding the seventh circle of the Inferno?" Death asked. "After he was defeated on Earth's plane he landed there, I thought. How can he be here? More important, why is he here and imprisoned? No one who runs the portals would allow something like him through."

"What are you talking about?" I said completely bewildered. "Who is in the seventh circle of the Inferno?"

Death actually said *tsk tsk*.

He said that out loud?

"I will have to talk to Thomas about inter-dimensional history classes again. The schools try to do a good job, I know, but there are still some large gaps. Didn't they ever have you read Dante's *Inferno?*

"I think I was out killing a few zombies that week," I muttered defensively. Reading was one of my favorite pastimes, but there always seemed to be one more book I hadn't read. I'm in high school and about to graduate in a few months - once I get through the prom and finals. I felt older than my years, however. Some of the things I had seen while banishing the spirits made me feel like I was centuries old. Still, I made a mental note to find that book.

"Maybe we should find a movie on it?" Death asked. "We could watch it and eat popcorn."

First he hinted at pancakes and now movie and popcorn. Was he asking me out on a date?

"I watch movies every Friday with my Uncle Jasper," I said a bit too primly. "Maybe we can add it to the list. But, right now, I think we have a little more pressing matters to get back to, don't you think?" Now I knew I sounded like a schoolmarm who was lecturing her students. I mentally cringed inside.

Death grinned at me, unrepentant. "Yah, we should probably do something. He'll cause more problems than we'll want to deal with."

The sound of twigs snapping on the other side of the mausoleum caused both of us to move farther back into the trees and hide within their shadows. I knew I wanted to see what or who was approaching. At this time of night, it could be anyone or anything. I reached down to get my iron knife and shut down my senses and could feel Death doing the same with his.

Four people in hooded robes began circling the mausoleum in a procession. Once there was one per side, chanting began. The words were strange to my ears, but I could feel Death straighten suddenly beside me. He leant down and put his lips on my ear and began telling me what they were saying.

Pasiphae's offspring,
Barbarous and wild.
Our arrow of wrath,
To claim our path,
Heed our call.
Three Nights of Hell,
We do foretell.

As that line was said, the mausoleum's edges began to glow a strange pulsating red-orange and the pounding of the Minotaur stopped. I knew it sensed freedom was at hand. Freedom to go out and lay waste and destruction on every living soul who got in its way.

"Obviously, this is the part where we need to step in," I said in a seemingly bright and cheerful tone. "Ready?"

"Sounds like fun. Do we have a plan or are we just winging this?"

"Plans are so overdone. It's much better to barge in and allow sarcasm to take control."

"Oh, wonderful." Death said and gave a drawn out long-suffering sigh. "Let's get to it. I don't want to miss this for anything."

I snorted and straightening my spine in a vain attempt to look taller. It helped me—mentally at least.

"Hey, guys," I said in a cheerful tone. "What's up?"

"This is sarcasm?" asked Death dryly. "I was expecting something a little more."

"Give me a second," I said. "I have to start with something to break the ice."

At my first words, the chanting hooded figures had stopped and turned towards us. Now, they pulled out a few knives. This was my first indication that they were not happy even though I couldn't see their faces. I was a bit relieved to see the glow begin to fade from the stone walls of the mausoleum.

"Now. Now. No need for violence. We can come to a rational and satisfaction conclusion for all this very easily. It all starts with you pulling down your hoods and putting away those knives. I hope you have clothes on under there. No need to scare the dead."

"I'm still waiting," Death said with a grin. "Would you like me to take a turn?"

Now it was my turn to sigh. "Sure. I guess I'm too tired to form a properly sarcastic retort right now."

"Time for all little acolytes to be in bed," he said to the figures. "Tonight's show just got canceled."

The figures came as one, ready for a fight. The Minotaur started his roars again as did the pounding.

"You keep them busy," I said. "I'm sending this bull guy home. Hopefully that means this seventh circle."

Death had two of the figures on the ground and out like a light before I even finished my sentence. The other two took positions in front and behind Death. This didn't seem to faze him in the least. In a roundhouse kick that momentarily distracted me from my own preparations—my God, that man had abs—he took out the one in front before turning to face the last remaining. As the figure flew at him with outstretched arms, Death grabbed one and allowed the figure's own momentum to assist in throwing him against the mausoleum's walls. The cracking sound wasn't just the crash of the body.

With a roar, one arm of the Minotaur punched through the stone.

"My time to shine," I muttered. Once more I raised my Sight and began my own chanting. Rather than try and contain the Minotaur, I believed—okay, make that I hoped—unraveling the pentagram would send him back to his circle. It was the only thing holding him to this plane.

The pentagram glowed every color of the rainbow in turn and sparks began to fly. Just in time. The Minotaur's head and shoulders were through the hole.

He was one ugly bull.

The pentagram broke with a loud pop and just as quickly the Minotaur was gone. It seemed anti-climactic, but I didn't care. I was grateful it was gone.

A large howl erupted behind us, and Death and I turned in time to see a hooded figure race towards the cemetery's exit.

"Should we follow?" I asked.

"I think we can start by questioning these four." Death pointed at the unconscious acolytes. "I'll get Thomas over here, and he can take them wherever he takes people."

"An Angel's job is never done." I smiled at Death.

"Pancakes?" he asked.

"Sure. Just let me run home and let my Uncle Jasper know. He sometimes worries. How about I meet you at the diner in an hour?"

"Sounds good," he said. "That will let me take care of getting Thomas here and that little task."

"That's right. The slightly…illegal act. What are you going to do? Rob a grave?"

Death fixed me with such an innocent look that I knew I had hit on it the first time out.

I began to shake my head and back away. "I don't want to know."

"But really…"

"No. As long as Thomas knows about it, I'm out of it. See you in a bit."

I left the cemetery and jogged the few blocks to my street. I slowed down as I walked around the corner and saw my house on its oversized lot. It always felt good to be home.

A brush of cold at my side had me see that Fog had joined me. It was silent tonight. Sometimes that's just how we were. Fog liked to see what was going on around Shadow Street.

My house looked like something out of Earth's Victorian era—which is where it had originally been before one of my ancestors had the bright idea of teleporting it over to Shadow Street while playing around with time travel and translocation. Needless to say, he got his hands slapped by the Guardian Council. Now, both are strictly forbidden. Um, well in my mind, if the Council doesn't know about it, I'm not going to say anything. After all, don't most of the families in Shadow Street have a few secrets? Mine has so many we took to writing them in a journal. As the proud owner of said journal, I knew most of them. I suspected Uncle Jasper had several, however, that he had never written down.

My thoughts were on my family's secrets and had been firmly ordered to not think about Death's perfect lips…and oh, they were perfect... Stop, I told myself for the tenth time. Perhaps if I had been concentrating on my surroundings and not Death's looks, I would have felt the presence behind me. But, I hadn't and it was a complete shock to have someone's arm wrap around my waist and a wet, smelly cloth pressed against my face. Before I could even struggle, I was out like a light.

The cold woke me up first. I was lying on a stone slab that felt rough against my back. Against my back? Suddenly, I knew with terrifying clarity I was lying on the altar wearing nothing. I could feel something across me and could only pray it covered the important spots. I couldn't move anything except my eyes, and what I saw didn't reassure me at all. This was not going to end well.

Above me, the Dusky Moon shone its weak light down. Enough light for me to see the hooded figures that circled around the altar. I didn't need the light to hear the *bleat* of a goat. This was definitely not going to end well. Not for me and not for the goat.

The robed figures began to chant then.

"Why do I suddenly feel like I'm in the middle of one of those B-movie that Jasper and I like to watch? How many of you acolytes are out there?" I wondered out loud.

"Silence," a voice thundered. "You have returned our master—our brother—to his circle. Now, you must be the sacrifice so that we may bring him back."

"You did such a good job in keeping him happy last time," I said. "I don't think he liked the accommodations. Besides, it wasn't like you really knew what to do with him. Talk about the black sheep…err bull of the family."

"Enough." That same voice interrupted me. "We have yet to find the missing fragment, but we will."

"Missing fragment?" I asked. No, I never will learn to keep my mouth shut.

Prepare the drink," the man commanded. I heard more rustling and then the goat began to *bleat* again.

"No," I cried. "I will not drink anything." I began to shout and rant about anything that came to mind but was silenced by a large hand across my mouth.

"Enough." The voice was full of frustration. The man began to chant and this time without Death to translate, I had no idea what he said.

The silver blade that appeared above me gave me more than a few moments pause. The sound of the leader's voice as he muttered the incantation creeped me out. I knew in my heart this time I wasn't going to escape and said my final prayers. For some reason, I was at peace with the idea of death although I was a little sad I hadn't been able to spend more time with Death. Despite the seriousness of the situation, a little giggle formed in my head with the play on words. I'm a weird person.

My attention was then transfixed by the descending blade, a bright blue spark, and then the dark and shadows surrounded me.

I awoke in Hell.

"Well this isn't where I expected to go to when I died. I'm not sure this is going to work out well for anyone."

A bellowing roar filled my ears and stopped my musing. I looked around and saw a very familiar figure in the distance. "This is definitely not going to work out well," I said with a heavy sigh for the third time that night.

I looked down and was relieved that even though I was dead I had some shift covering me. Barely. Naked and I didn't work out well in public.

"Only you would be happy about something like that at a time like this," I said. "At least we managed to send it back where it belonged. I'm not sure where that leaves me in all this. I am dead, aren't I?"

"Kind of." That voice was familiar, too.

I turned around in relief and again found myself face to chest with Death. "Not that I'm not happy to see you," I said with a bit of relief, "but what are we doing here? Am I dead?"

"Let's just say you are straddling the line between the living and the dead. We have to say thank you to Fog. It came and found me after the cult grabbed you. You'll be okay. I'm here." He followed that with a quick peck on the tip of my nose. He seemed to like doing that.

"Well, I have no desire to stay. I thought I died when that guy was doing that thing with the knife and the silly chanting." Somehow, that came out a bit garbled. *You don't have to make sense*, I consoled myself. *You're kinda dead.*

Death laughed. "Let's just say I borrowed you for a little bit. It's going to be okay. I didn't have more than a minute to react, which is why we're here. But they should be gone now. We'll have to have a talk with Thomas about what to do about this cult. That can wait though. Let's get out of here. Then we can go get pancakes. I'm starving."

"You and those pancakes. Okay. We get out of here, and it's a deal." I stopped myself before the word date came out. Well, almost.

Death smiled at me, and I could tell by the look in his eyes he knew full well what I almost said.

The bellows began again and this time we both looked to see the Minotaur standing on a broken slope. Something below him had caught his attention and thankfully, it wasn't us.

A spark of blue and I was on the altar again. This time, no one was brandishing a blade over me. I sat up and clutched the sheet that covered me.

The next thing I knew, I was picked up with strong arms and the sheet was pulled around me in a toga-like fashion. At least it kept my modesty intact.

Still, I felt positively naked standing there next to him.

"Did I really die?" I asked in a voice that was a little too wobbly for my taste. *Hey, I was a Keeper. I should take this stuff in stride.* Then I broke all the rules and snuggled into Death's embrace for comfort.

The *bleat* of the goat interrupted the moment.

"Oh, good. It's alive. What are we going to do with it though?" I asked.

"We could give it to Baba Yaga at the diner," Death suggested. "I'll bet she could make a mean goat curry." He laughed, and then wheezed when my fist connected with his stomach. His nice hard and flat stomach I found out.

"Hey, I was just joking," he protested. "I don't know what to do with a goat. Can you keep him as a pet?"

"I'd sooner have a Hellhound than a goat," I said. "At least they are housebroken. I think. We'll take him over to Cinere and Corvus. They'll find a nice place for him."

"Well, get dressed. I need pancakes."

I gathered the sheet and as much of my dignity together as I could and scurried behind the destroyed and broken mausoleum and changed into my clothes. For some odd reason, they were at the edge of the walkway folded in a nice neat pile. I didn't want to question that one.

I almost screamed when something cold and wet brushed my bare behind and whirled around. It was Fog.

I reached out and gave it a pat somewhere within its misty depths and was rewarded with one of its rare words.

"Safe."

"Thanks to you and Death," I said. "It's not everyday I can say I was rescued by an Elemental and a Grim Reaper."

It wrapped itself around my arm and for a brief moment, I had a glimpse of Fog's mind and what I saw both enthralled and spooked me. Then, it drew back and began to wind itself away to the other side of the cemetery.

And so, Death and I and one very-upset-but-at-least-not-sacrificed goat left the cemetery and went to eat pancakes. Even the goat had some. After all, no one can say no to Shadow Street's Blueberry Pancakes.

INANNA'S RAGE
The Cemetery
by Morgan Ashe

No! It couldn't be true.

I had to turn my head away as unrelenting panic entered my body. I could feel it start at my toes and blossom upward until a hard knot formed in my stomach. My lips curled back and my teeth bared in a silent scream. I was frozen.

What will I do?

No Ben and Jerry's Chunky Monkey. My absolute-must-have-Friday-night ice cream. That wonderful banana ice cream with fudge chunks and walnuts.

I stood there with the freezer door open. The mist from the ice cream section rolled around each pint and billowed toward me. Ben and Jerry's Coffee, Triple Carmel Chunk, Butter Pecan...nope, no Chunky Monkey. A tag indicated the row where it belonged, but even a search through the adjoining pints yielded not a single one of that luscious, decadent treat.

"How am I supposed to watch TV tonight without my ice cream?" I muttered.

"Get the Cherry Garcia," a voice whispered behind me.

Too busy searching, I said without turning around, "No, I want Chunky Monkey."

Suddenly, I felt a distinct cold breeze along my back. Goose bumps rose on the skin that was exposed above my pants. Realizing that this was different than the cold I felt from the cooler, I began to look around just as the voice whispered again, "Get the Cherry Garcia."

I could feel a prickle of electricity in the air. I turned completely and saw a full-bodied apparition standing in front of me. It was a gray haired man with a bushy beard and mustache. Round eyeglasses finished off his face giving him the appearance of a happy Santa Claus. Except Santa wouldn't have been caught dead in a tie-dyed bandana and T-shirt. He looked familiar. I leaned forward to get a closer look.

Oh. My. God. It was Jerry Garcia. *The* Jerry Garcia. Well, the dead one anyway. I didn't even question the fact that a legend from Earth's history was appearing in this dimension. Too many weird things had been happening with the gates lately that I no longer questioned anything. As long as this market kept getting Ben and Jerry's in somehow, I didn't care to get a headache trying to figure it out. "So what happened, Jerry? Heaven's psychedelic band didn't need you for a front man so you became a rep for Ben and Jerry's?"

"You can see me?" he asked.

"Clear as mud…um…ectoplasm," I replied.

"Aren't you a cheeky monkey?"

"One tries," I said modestly. "It's not every day you meet an icon from Earth's history in the ice cream aisle of the Shadow Street Grocery Mart. At least not for me."

We discussed music for several minutes. Then the conversation began to get a little more intense.

"It's pretty clear now that what looked like some kind of counterculture is, in reality, just the plain old chaos of undifferentiated weirdness," he argued.

Oh great, Jerry is actually quoting himself. I've heard that line before. Here I am at eight p.m. on a Friday night discussing Earth's esoteric sixties social consciousness with a dead man. I began to notice some odd stares from other shoppers as they walked by watching me talk to myself. Then again, this was Shadow Street. Who can say what's weird? If they knew who my friends were and what I did for a living those stares would hold fear instead of just idle curiosity.

I needed to cut this conversation short and so interrupted his monologue on the consciousness of music and the universality of the guitar. "Jerry, it's been a real pleasure, but I have to get going. Maybe we'll meet again in the ice cream aisle someday."

He nodded and gave me his signature peaceful grin. "Get the Cherry Garcia, it's always the number one flavor. For a reason." And with that, he disappeared.

Shaking my head in wonder, I turned back to my quest for the Holy Chunky Monkey Grail. An entire row of the coveted ice cream was stacked in front of me where none had stood before. I smiled briefly before grabbing a pint and turned, only to find someone else blocking my way. Like Jerry's ghost, I could see right through this presence as well.

"Jasper. I thought I told you to wait in the car. You know what happens when you spend too much time in stores. Remember the *Popping Candy Cane Incident?* Or, the *Let's See How Many Cans of Vegetables Could Fall Off the Shelves at Once Incident?*"

My Great-Uncle Jasper may have been dead for the last seventy years, but he is one of my favorite people. Every Friday evening we watch old movies and eat ice cream. I know what you're thinking. But yes, he can still eat ice cream for some reason, and Chunky Monkey has been *our* flavor for the last year. He stood there, visible only to me, wearing a T-shirt that said "Ghosts Do It in the Dark". With baggy shorts and scruffy boat shoes, he looked like he belonged somewhere on a beach rather than the middle of a store in Shadow Street. The T-shirt would change weekly, but I had never seen him without those shorts and shoes.

"I know, Rebekah, but I was getting bored and you said you'd only be gone for five minutes, and I want to stop and talk to a few people before we watch the movie."

"We are not stopping by the cemetery. You remember what happened last time we went there, don't you? My luck and we'll wind up spending another night with that silly mortician Milton Mortimer. Yeesh. Uncle Jas—" The high pitched squeal of the overhead loudspeaker interrupted me.

"Clean up needed in aisle five and aisle six."

Uh oh, time to get out of here.

"Come on, Jasper. Go get in the car while I pay for this." I turned and began walking toward the checkout counter.

"Oooohhhh, wait." I heard him say. "Cherry Garcia."

Or did he say Jerry?

I didn't turn around. I just kept walking and picked up a few candy bars and some bags of dried cherries as I went.

I paid for the treats and walked out to the almost deserted parking lot that ran along Shadow and Main. A red glow emanated for a second near the cemetery walls and the ever-present Fog seemed thicker than usual. The night's quiet was broken by the haunting howl of a dog. A Hellhound. The hairs on the back of my neck rose, and I almost jumped out of my skin as Jasper materialized next to me.

"What's happening over there, Jasper? You didn't mention any of this."

Jasper started to look a bit nervous, and I could swear I saw a trickle of sweat bead down the side of his face.

"No-nothing," he stuttered, and then a look of fear flashed across his face. "Today is the 18th right?"

"It's the 19th. Why? What does the date matter?" As I looked at him, he grew even more transparent and flickered in and out of this plane a few times before settling into his usual milky white form. "Jasper, what do you know? Tonight after midnight is the spring equinox but nothing else except for some planned sabbats."

"No, after midnight tonight she will be released if someone doesn't stop it."

"She?" I replied turning towards him. "I've never felt anyone else's presence there. Who are you talking about?"

"The Queen of the Sky. Daughter of the sky god Anu. She is known as Inanna."

"Inanna," I questioned. "She's the goddess of love and war. War. Are you telling me she's coming here? How is that possible? She's locked in the Ninth Dimension with Lumiel. And you were planning on telling me this when?"

"Um…tomorrow. It's Friday night, and that movie I've been waiting for arrived today. Plus we've been out of Chunky Monkey for days."

"Oh sure, let impending death and destruction build up while we enjoy ice cream and a movie?" Now that his initial fear had subsided, I noticed Jasper didn't even have the grace to look abashed. He merely looked at his shorts and plucked at a non-existent ectoplasmic piece of lint.

I sighed and pulled my cell phone out of my jeans and pushed a few buttons to call my supervisor. For the past five years I'd worked for Shadow Keepers. For hundreds of years this group was all that had stood between the evil that lurked in and under Shadow Street. Keepers who struggled to take Shadow Street back and ensure that which was spawned in this area would stay confined within its boundaries, keeping the world safe from harm. The current Keepers were a motley group of ghosts, necromancers, and spirit binders. I fell into the latter of the three categories although I had a few talents up my sleeve I didn't talk about, even with the Keepers. I was the youngest Keeper they had ever had, but I wasn't so young I didn't know how to keep my mouth shut. After what I'd seen in the last five years I always thought the minimum age should be fifty to join because it was such a hair-raising experience.

After a brief, unsatisfactory discussion with Jackson, my supervisor, I hung up. How he had become a supervisor I have no idea. They say cream always rises to the top. Obviously scum does, too.

"Jasper, you have to find your own transportation home. Just do that quick skip across planes of existence you do. I have to go to the cemetery. Jackson is sending backup."

"Rebeeeekkkaaahhhh," he whined. "Let them handle it. I really want to watch that movie. I've waited forever for it."

"Go, Jasper. Now. We'll do it tomorrow night, 'kay?"

With a huff—who knew ghosts could huff—Jasper blinked out of sight, and I could start towards the cemetery. I tossed the ice cream in the trashcan by the door and went to confront Inanna. Eating ice cream would have been so much better.

So here I stood at midnight waiting, cloaked by the boughs of several pines, safe from the dim glow of a solitary streetlight. Its glow barely shone enough to illuminate the sidewalk below. Ambient light from the full moon silhouetted trees and buildings against the night sky, even that was dimmed by the swirling Fog rolling in where the base of Shadow Street met the dark, dank waters of the river. Fortunately I had night vision like a *Fumi*.

The slight breeze did nothing to dispel the musty scent that seemed to pervade every breath I took. Under the fragrant spicy tang of the pines lurked another. One with a faint odor of decay and mustiness that no wind could push away. Shadow Street had too many memories, too many skeletons buried for anything to cleanse that smell from its foundations.

I turned towards the library and the inside lights shut off. Inside and out, the library plunged into darkness. Two green glowing orbs burned for a moment in one of the smoky glass doors before fading. My skin prickled into goose bumps, and a shiver went down my spine.

Wonder what is in there? Another day, another night, I promised myself.

Not tonight, however. Tonight I had another destination. Not the library, not the church across the street. No, tonight I was focused on what was inside of the tall iron gates and stone walls attached to the side of the church. I had never understood walls around a cemetery, until a few years ago, when I was sixteen. A harrowing evening that made me realize cemetery walls were there not to keep people out, but to keep its occupants in. Then there was the incident last week on the other side of the cemetery. Another set of problems that needed to be resolved. We still had no idea who was behind the cult, and, we needed to find out sooner rather than later.

Shadows from the iron rails of the gate stretched out—across the sidewalk and street like spindly fingers reaching out to beckon any passersby, daring them to look between the gaps and scroll-work and come inside. One lone, twisted and gnarled, ancient oak stood sentinel over faded markers and granite Angels kneeling in perpetual tears and unending prayers.

Tonight was like no other around the cemetery. I had walked past those gates a thousand times but had never felt this. Souls screaming. Screaming to be free, to hunt, to consume. Screaming to escape the bonds that tied them to that place. Overriding that was another soul, ancient and evil, that was feeding off their emotions. Growing stronger.

I silently cursed Jasper for not talking about this sooner. Our previous visits to the cemetery were to talk to old friends of his who hadn't wanted to pass over.

Even at this distance I could feel the hatred of her ancient soul rolling out, washing my skin and senses with a tingling sea of her rage. I began to sweat as the anxiety built inside of me, increasing my heart rate. My guards had been down too long. I raised them, protecting my mind from the nightmares waiting to enter.

I caught a movement from the corner of my eye and whirled, my body immediately going to full crouch, an iron blade in one hand, a fistful of salt in my other. Yeah, yeah. I know—salt—but pound for pound, I will stick to tried and true when faced with the unknown over a mystical spell any day. Plus, it's cheap and with Jasper's love for movies and ice cream I saved every penny I could. Keeper duty doesn't come with a large paycheck.

Death stood in front of me, a faint smile on his face. A face that belied countless decades of reaping souls and sending them on their way. With those blue eyes and a rakish five o'clock shadow, he looked like he should be a model. His jeans, though... I looked at the stonewashed jeans that hugged his narrow hips and noticed the grass stain on one knee.

"Football? At a time like this?" I smirked at him as I straightened and drew closer.

"What can I say, the Angels had an unfair advantage. Thomas decided to take a break and play on the Guardian's side so the Reapers needed a little help."

"Do I need to ask who won? Or whether it was fair?"

"Not my fault if a few feathers were ruffled. Thomas should learn to tuck them in a bit tighter." With a flourish, he drew a single, perfect gray feather from his pocket. Its glow, edges outlined by a white light tinged with blue, chased back the shadows surrounding us and illuminated Death's features. His eyes twinkled with mischievous glee, and he gave me a slow wink before offering the feather to me.

"Keep it safe, never know when an Enochian's feather is needed."

"I'm surprised it isn't a black one of yours. Not that you keep your wings visible." I took the feather from his fingers and felt a small tingle of electricity arc between us. It took me back to a week ago, during *The Death before Drinking Goat's Blood Incident*, when we had touched for the first time. Whether it was from our touch or the feather I didn't know, and now was not the time to find out. I slipped the feather into the pocket of my jacket, hoping it wouldn't get too crushed. I looked up to find Death staring at me with more than merriment in his eyes.

"I've wondered what would happen when we touched, again. Whether that first time was a quirk," he said. He touched one of the soft ruffled cuffs at my wrists.

"These are pretty. They look hand knitted."

I, too, reached down and stroked my fingers over the soft cashmere. "Corvus made them for me last week. She and Cinere wanted to hear more about the cult and asked me over for tea. If you look closely, there are iron beads knitted into them. A girl can't have enough iron or salt around in her opinion. Of course their silly, *Fumus* got hair all over them, but that adds to the charm I think. Plus, they look great with leather and blue jeans." Realizing I was babbling, I shut up and then nervously pulled down the sleeves of my jacket to keep my hands occupied.

It didn't help. Death leaned in closer, and closer, and then a bit closer.

Despite my reservations, I started to tilt my head forward, but just before our lips touched a piercing howl filled the air. We both turned to face the street and there, standing at the gates of the cemetery, stood a hound—a Hellhound by the size of it. It stood, back to us and lifted its head to deliver another spine tingling, chilling howl.

"I heard him earlier. Shouldn't he be howling at the living? Nothing is alive in there, at least not that I can sense."

Death looked as puzzled as I. The crisp odor of ozone tickled my nose as Death opened his senses. Lowering my shields didn't help. There was nothing sentient in that graveyard. Not yet anyway. I felt only the rage and despair I had felt earlier.

"What is he howling at?" I asked.

"I'm almost afraid to find out." Death's attention was focused squarely at something inside the cemetery. He gave a sharp whistle, and the Hellhound's ears pricked up. It froze for a second and spun around to race towards us. He came between us rubbing his head against Death's jeans and then leaned into me. I'd never been this close to a Hellhound. He was hot, almost burning to the touch and little wisps of smoke curled up from his nostrils. He nuzzled against the pocket of my jacket while excited yips issued from his throat.

I heard the crinkly noise and knew what he wanted. "No, that's my dinner," I told him. "You can't have it." His cries became more insistent and the smoke intensified. I even saw wisps starting to escape from his pricked up ears.

"Aren't they supposed to eat flesh or carrion or something?" I asked Death.

"Are you going to say no to a Hellhound?" he replied. He raised his eyebrow and gave me that cocky grin that caused my heart to melt.

I gave a loud sigh and, reaching in my pocket, pulled out a candy bar.

"What was dinner tonight?"

"A Whatchamacallit and some dried cherries." I sighed while peeling the wrapper open. "It was supposed to be ice cream with Jasper."

"Oh yeah, it's Friday night. Jasper asked me over, but then Jackson called. He couldn't find anyone else available," Death replied.

"You do know dogs are not supposed to have chocolate, don't you?" I asked.

"This isn't a dog. This is a Hellhound, and I think he's adopted you."

"Why is he being friendly with us? Shouldn't he be attacking?"

A long line of drool was already oozing from the Hellhound's mouth in anticipation of the treat. I could hear it sizzle as it hit the cement sidewalk. I tried offering him some dried cherries but was greeted with an upturned nose while his gaze never wavered from my favorite candy bar. I gave another loud sigh and took the candy out of the wrapper and gave it to the Hellhound. It was gone in an instant, and his gaze immediately fixated on my pocket.

"No. No, more. One is enough."

As if he understood an almost disappointed look came into his eyes.

"Yup," said Death, "he's yours now. You'll have to take him for walks and get him a bowl and feed him regularly. I'm going to enjoy watching this. What are you going to call him?"

"You have got to be kidding me, right? What am I going to do with a Hellhound? Shouldn't he be going back home to…well…Hell or wherever they are from? And what's Jasper going to say? You know he has issues with dogs. They love to race through him and scatter his molecules."

"He'll have to deal with it. I'll talk to him if that will help. Once you feed Hellhounds, they're yours forever, smoke and all."

At the word smoke, the Hellhound turned towards Death, alert.

"There you go. His name must be Smoke, he recognized it." With that, Death started making kissy faces at the Hellhound and acting uncharacteristically strange even for him. "Is that your name? Smoke? Smokie? That's it. Smokie. What a good lil' doggie you are." My new Hellhound, apparently called Smokie, stood there whipping his tail back and forth like an idiot and the two bonded right there in the middle of Shadow Street.

"You have got to be kidding me. We have more important things to look into tonight. Get a hold of yourself. What's next? A game of fetch?"

"Actually, Smokie would probably enjoy chasing down a goat or two. Think there are any around here? It is a witch's Sabbat after all. Ostara ceremonies are so much fun to watch." Death looked at me with a devil-may-care grin.

Throwing my hands up in surrender, I turned my attention back to the cemetery. Whatever the Hellhound—no, make that Smokie—had been howling at was either gone or hidden from my Sight.

I started walking across the street—deserted by even Shadow Street standards—and found myself flanked on either side by Death and Smokie. I wasn't sure if Smokie was on that side for the potential candy bar in my pocket or because he was protecting me. The latter made me feel a bit more secure. When faced with the unknown, the more on my side, the merrier.

We reached the gates, their rusted and flaking iron spines topped by wicked sharp spikes stretching into the night sky, towered over us. The ornate carvings didn't block our view of the interior of the cemetery.

"So Jackson told me a little about what's happening," Death told me. "I asked him twice why no one knew of her rising tonight and all I got in reply was muttering about conjunction dates and lost passages being misread. I asked him why the resident entrails reader hadn't foreseen it, but he said she's been having difficulties after the incident with the two goats and the farmer last month. Good readers are so hard to find, I tell you. Jackson is an idiot, though. I'll have to talk to Thomas about him."

"Funny, he went into mutter-mode with me, too, when I asked him that same question," I replied. "I only caught words like electrolytes, imbalance, and goats. I wish I'd been at that ceremony with the reader."

"Shouldn't they have sent more than the two of us?"

"I think he sent the others to clear everyone they could away from the danger."

"His usual optimistic self. All right. You ready?"

"Yep, let's go."

As if they knew what we were saying, the gates swung inward with a screeching, grinding noise.

We looked at each other, and Death shrugged before bowing to me. "Normally, fair lady, I would say ladies first, but in this case, please allow me." He straightened and strode through the gates.

I snorted and followed him in, Smokie at my heels. For a Hellhound he was being uncharacteristically quiet. Not that I'd been around any of them, but I'd always thought of them as fierce and wild. He must have been the runt of his litter.

The graves hadn't been landscaped for a long time. Weeds and vines trailed around the headstones. One plot of land actually looked like it had been freshly dug. The dirt was piled next to the open pit, a shovel lying next to it as if the gravedigger had been interrupted half way through. I had to wonder who or what had done that.

The ever-present mist and Fog playing at our feet gave the area tops in the creep factor for me. Fog came up behind us and I heard his raspy voice say one word. "Careful."

I have never felt comfortable in cemeteries, but tonight was one of the eeriest. I should never have listened to Jasper. I should have studied cosmetology or fashion design. I looked down at my faded jeans and scuffed boots. Who was I kidding? This was the perfect job for me.

Crinkle. Crinkle.

I turned at the noise and found Smokie licking an empty bag of what had held chocolate-covered pretzels. "Smokie! Get away from there. You are so lucky the chocolate is going to kill you before I do," I hissed at him. "This is no time for that. Jeez."

"There is always time for a snack, or…" Death leaned over and gave me a kiss. Not a fast peck either. It was slow and lingering and… Well, enough of that for now. We had a goddess to banish. I gave it one more second before reluctantly pulling away from him, tingles still rippling through me. Then I realized, the tingles weren't all coming from Death.

There. In front of us a red cloud full of sparks and flashes of lightning was coalescing, spreading out until a large circle formed.

A portal? Here?

"This is impossible," I said. "There has never been a portal here." I looked at Death, and he looked a bit stunned himself.

"Well, this is new," he said. "I'm sure Thomas will enjoy this little story later."

"If we survive it," I said.

From the depths of the cloud, a woman stalked out. She was dressed in the manner of ancient Sumerian warriors. A bronze helmet covered most of her head, her long black hair escaping from it into a riotous mass around her face and shoulders. She carried a shield and spear and a leopard spotted cape was clasped around her neck. Her feet were shod in laced sandals, and leather studded armor covered her torso to finish the look. She made a terrifying and imposing figure.

Death blew out a breath from between his pursed lips and quietly said, "Well, the first thing we have to do is take her shopping. That outfit is so yesterday."

Despite the tenseness of the situation and impending death and destruction about to rain down at us, I had to take a second to chuckle before replying, "Shoes first, please, and don't let the Shadow Street Humane Society see that cape or we'll all be mauled."

With our words, Inanna's gaze fixed on us and a cruel smile curled her upper lip. "Kneel before me, my little chickens. My time has come to rise and return to power. My armies are already gathering to attack. I have waited long for this."

"Umm…did she just refer to us as fowl? Like some type of sacrificial fodder?" I half turned to Death. In spite of the ghosts in the cemetery crying out in fear from Inanna's presence, I was finding it very hard to take any of this seriously. In fact, the whole thing seemed anti-climactic. "We waited an hour for this? I was expecting world destruction at the very least. Jackson is going to hear about this. In fact, the only thing I'm wondering about is how that portal was formed."

Inanna screamed in rage and threw her spear towards Death. He dodged and came back kicking out at her. For being so awkwardly dressed, she did a nice variation of a roundhouse kick, catching Death in the side and taking him down to the ground. He grunted in surprise. She walked over to him and gave him a quick kick in the ribs before turning her attention to me. With a sweep of her arm, she backhanded me in a careless gesture. I landed at her feet in the dirt next to a grave I recognized. For a second I swear I could see a shaking, nervous ghostly figure before it disappeared. "I'll remember your help, Milton. Yeesh."

Behind Inanna, the growing vortex eddied and flowed with blood-red furls reaching out from the center. It was growing second by second.

Skeleton armies waited impatiently in the center for it to expand so they could enter into our plane and begin their nightmare battles. I began to wonder though, as the leader seemed to argue with several warriors behind him. It looked like unrest was advancing through the ranks. I'm not sure why, and I hoped we could end this before finding out.

Inanna stood over me, and like Smokie had done earlier, raised her head to the night sky and howled. Hers was a scream of victory and triumph.

Death looked over at me, grimacing from the last blow. "Now may be a good time to use that little present I brought you tonight."

Illumination filled my mind, and I realized it was all meant to be. I smiled at Death and drew the feather from my pocket. It was perfect, untouched by the fight. I reached out to her with it, and a burning glow of electricity crackled between the feather and her leg. The smell of charred flesh wafted across my nose.

Faster than I could see, Death jacked himself up and threw himself against her. A blur to my right, and then Smokie was in focus as he launched into a leap and hit Inanna directly in her chest. She staggered back several feet. Their continued blows and kicks drove her back farther and farther. Suddenly, two skeletal hands wrapped themselves around her neck and pulled her into the maelstrom and into the bony embrace of her army. They fell upon her as her screams of pure rage rent the air. The currents flowed inward upon themselves and with a pop, disappeared as a blinding light ignited around us. The sound of the lone oak splitting in two was followed by a thunderous crash. Death landed on his butt next to me, a hot and sprawled Smokie across our laps. Of course, now that the danger was past, he took an opportunity to sniff my pocket again. I gave him a hug. He'd helped save the day. Heck, he'd helped save Shadow Street. "We'll get you a dozen candy bars, Smokie. Just give us a minute to catch our breaths."

"That's it? Did we kill her or only put her back to her dimension?" I wondered aloud. A feeling of disappointment swept through me. It had been too easy.

"Does it really matter?" Death's question caused me to reopen my Sight. No longer did the screams and cries from the dead echo in my mind. Gone was that underlying feeling of rage and fury that had resonated from here.

A second later, a softly glowing gray feather drifted down in front of us. I looked at Death, and we burst out laughing. I heaved a reluctant Smokie away from me and stood.

Death stood and brushed off first my jeans, lingering a little bit over the interesting parts, and then his own. He straightened and wrapped his arms around me for a minute. We stood like that for a moment, and it felt right. But then the mood was broken by the sound of a tummy grumble. We chuckled and moved apart. I bent and picked up the feather.

"That was the nicest thing you ever gave me."

"I can think of several things that will be better. But we'll leave that for later. I'm hungry. Pancakes?"

Smokie looked first at Death—obviously keying in on the word pancakes, although how a Hellhound knows what they are is beyond me—and then at me before racing toward the gates.

Death jogged over to the gravestones and picked up Inanna's spear before returning and threading his cold fingers through mine—that same tingle that I'd felt before skittered across my skin. "Jasper will like this, I think."

"Do you think she'll come back?" I questioned.

"If it's not her, it will be something else. We will have to meet with Thomas later and figure out what is happening. Something has been off around here for the past few months. We need to figure it out."

"We will," I replied, only half believing my own words. "But right now what matters is getting a nice stack of pancakes from the Shadow Street Diner and another Whatchamacallit or two for Smokie."

The two of us turned and left the cemetery and began the walk to the Shadow Street Diner, while Smokie moved to my side, his hot nose against my hand offsetting Death's cool clasp.

I turned back and looked at the gates one last time. I knew she wasn't gone. She was still there, standing beyond the gates. Waiting. Watching. Biding her time. But I will be here, also. Guarding Shadow Street. Waiting. Watching. And boy was Jackson going to get a piece of my mind.

THE PEANUT BUTTER ON THE ROOF OF A HELLHOUND'S MOUTH INCIDENT
Beka's House
by Morgan Ashe

"For the love of all that is holy, Beka, you don't even have tuna fish?"

I watched as Death went from one cupboard to another, peering into each for a second before slamming the door and moving on.

"Nope."

"Bacon?"

"Over my dead body. Cheese and peanut butter are good sources of protein."

"Protein is supposed to be meat, not nuts and berries." Death shuddered and moved on to the refrigerator.

"Not when you're a vegetarian, and technically peanuts are a legume, not a nut."

"This is not the time for a lesson in botany. And what is a legume? Never mind. I don't want to know. You just got a Hellhound. You will have to feed him something."

"If I remember correctly, he's already consumed three Whatchamacallits and a stack of blueberry pancakes from the Shadow Street Diner. A very large stack. How hungry can he be?"

"You have Oreos, peanut butter, and celery. Mustard? Why do you have mustard? Actually, why are the cookies in the refrigerator? How do you survive? Never mind. I don't want to know that, either." Death pulled out the peanut butter and Oreos and placed them on the counter and began opening drawers. Presumably in search of a knife.

"Where is Jasper?" Death asked, and popped an Oreo into his mouth.

"Out with Lola. He mentioned something about a dance contest at the Senior Center. I'm not sure how he's going to react to Smokie. He hates how dogs run through him and scatter his ectoplasm. I suppose he'll be okay with the hound as long as Smokie stays off his favorite chair. You do know that is not how you eat an Oreo, right?" I asked, turning away as I spoke. It was hard to concentrate while watching Death's incredible mouth. The man was dangerous.

Smokie was sitting next to the back door, his gaze fixated on the counter. His body was the stillest I had seen for the past several hours. Of course helping to banish an ancient goddess and getting a new owner did take a certain amount of calories. Still, he had eaten more pancakes than even Death.

"What's an Oreo?" Thomas asked from the couch.

I jumped, startled at the sound of his voice in time to watch him solidify into his full corporeal form. I looked at the Angel in abject horror. Even Death looked appalled.

"You've never had an Oreo? How can you live in Heaven and not have Oreos? It can't be Heaven without Oreos." I was in complete denial. Everyone needed to have had an Oreo at least once.

"We do have peanut butter there if it's any consolation. Are Oreos good?"

"Um...if you put peanut butter on them it is food for the gods. The uses for peanut butter are endless." I looked over just in time to see what was the equivalent as the coming of the Four Horsemen of the Apocalypse.

"Oh, sweet Nine Gates of Hell. What are you doing? Noooo. Stop."

It all seemed to happen in slow motion from my perspective. I would later swear I watched the Oreo tumble and flip over itself like the slow-motion replay of a football moving towards the uprights during a field goal. I made an instinctive move to intercept, but knew in my heart it was too late.

With a casual jump, Smokie snatched the Oreo, dredged with a ginormous dollop of peanut butter. For one moment, everything looked fine. Then, much to Death's dismay, my horror, and Thomas' amusement, it started.

Smokie's jaws stopped in mid-chew and his large, pink tongue began to frantically twist and turn, trying to lick the roof of his mouth. I watched as he crashed into the side of the coffee table. The vase and figurine - gifts from Great Aunt Agatha - fell to the floor. The figurine landed head first on the vase breaking both into several large pieces. *Well at least I can blame it all on the Hellhound*, I thought not unhappily, momentarily distracted from the primary issue.

Smokie stumbled again and fell to the floor. He rolled for a moment before coming to rest on his back, his legs stretching towards the ceiling. The runes etched into his skin began to glow hotter and hotter until they were blue with spirit heat. I wondered if he was going to set the house on fire, but the heat seemed contained to his body. His tongue never stopped trying to scrape the peanut butter off the ridged surface of the roof of his mouth. His large white teeth snapped at the air in between tongues swipes. Their clicks and clacks could be heard over Thomas' guffaws.

"Do something," I demanded.

"What? I'm not putting my hand next to those teeth. He's enjoying it—let him be," Death said.

"Let him be? He'll destroy the entire house in a minute."

Finally, Smokie stopped. For a moment, I wondered if the heat of his body had helped melt the peanut butter. Hellhound physics. Something I'd ponder later. Smokie stood and shook himself, then looked over at Death. Even from where I stood, I could see his desire for more.

"Don't. You. Dare," I warned Death.

"Aww, come on. That was fun."

I sighed. Day one with a Hellhound. Life was going to be very interesting from here on with my new pet.

I shrugged and then smiled and picked up an Oreo. Twisting each wafer, I carefully separated them so the ooey-gooey goodness of the cream center was exposed. It was time to teach Thomas the true way to eat one.

THE LAST PENNY
The Spring
by Morgan Ashe

2 pennies to go…

"I'm telling you. Stop giving that dog chocolate. What's the matter with you? You're just feeding his habit and teaching him bad habits."

The girl sounded exasperated to Alison. She shifted on the slate outcropping, waiting for the visitors to come into view. They were several meters out but getting closer. The rock felt warm from the day's sun shining on it, a contrast to the cool evening air but not as warm as the water where her feet were submerged to the ankles. She crinkled her toes a little, scattering the tiny fish swimming in the spring's waters. Their small, darting bodies barely caused a ripple on the surface.

"Do you want to be the one to cut off his candy bar supply? Remember the *Outdoor Chocolatier's Demonstration Incident* last week? You're the one he sleeps with. Do you want to wake up with his face staring into yours?" the man said in a deep voice.

"What are you talking about? He does that already. Every time he wants something, in fact. He has no issue with bowling me over and standing on me until I give him what he wants."

"You have a point. Still, he's a Hellhound, not a dog. Let him have it. It's not hurting him."

"Fine. Here, you 'lil sneak, enjoy it. It's my last one." The crinkly sound of a wrapper filled the night.

"You love him, stop complaining," the man said.

"Hush. Did you really have to say that out loud? You want him more spoiled than he already is? But, yes, he is kind of growing on me."

Their friendly banter made Alison smile. They sounded fun. A movement caught her eye and she turned to watch Cassia swim past, her long, wet hair sleeked back against her head. She moved quietly and then disappeared under the long branches of the weeping willow that draped into the spring's waters. The Oceanid was careful never to be seen when people were around. Unlike Alison, she was not hidden from their gaze, not invisible to curious onlookers. Alison chewed her lower lip, worried about her friend. She didn't know what she could do for her.

Poor Cassia, even this beautiful evening probably failed to bring her comfort. And it was a beautiful evening. The Sparkling Moon cast its reflected light on the glade and the spring's waters sparkled and danced in tune with the slight breeze. Cicadas hummed in every direction, the sound waxing and waning like a living entity, growing silent as the voices rose louder during their lull. She lifted her face to the ebony sky and breathed in the sweet smell of the night, lush with the fragrance of summer's grasses and flowers.

The sound of voices interrupted her appreciation of the nightfall. "Tell me why we're out here again in the middle of nowhere at four a.m. when I should be getting some sleep? I have a test tomorrow, well today, in chemistry. It's mid-terms at last, and I need to go shopping for the prom. I can't believe I said I'd go with you."

"Beka, the prom experience is something not to be missed. I can't believe you weren't going. You need a well rounded life to balance your...er...extracurricular activities. I'll bet you've never sat on the beach and just watched the flames from a campfire while telling scary tales either."

"You mean raging ex-goddesses, Hellhounds, and Friday evenings watching movies with my great uncle Jasper the Ghost aren't enough? Oh, and the occasional four a.m. stroll with a guy I only know as Death? Are you suggesting I need puppies and rainbows and proms, too? What's next, getting excited about a new pair of shoes?"

"You have two months before the prom. Stop obsessing. Why can't—?"

"Smokie!" the girl interrupted the man. "Get out of that water, you idiot. You remember what happened last week when I tried to give you a bath. You created so much steam it rained in my bathroom."

Noisy splashing and, strangely, what sounded like hissing to Alison replaced the voices.

A large gray, soaking wet—oh-my-God-that-can't-be-a-dog-it's-the-size-of-a-barn—animal leapt up on the rock with Alison and stared down at her with blue glowing eyes. *Blue?* she thought. Even growing up in Shadow Street, she had never seen a Hellhound in person. Weren't they supposed to be deadly? There were blue glowing runes etched into his skin and wisps of smoke drifted from his nostrils while more tendrils curled from his fur. He gave a quick shake and sent droplets of water through the air. Each one stood out separately, almost frozen in time for a moment, glistening with the moon's light. Then a wet, hot nose pressed into Alison's face and the beast—Smokie, she surmised—began licking her cheek. "Eww," she said, holding out a hand to push him away. One final lick and he was gone, splashing back to the other side of the spring and the couple who were almost at its edge.

"Smokie... Don't. You. Dare. Stop," the man warned, but it was too late. Just as he had to her, the Hellhound shook and rained water droplets over both the man and the woman. Beka shrieked and jumped back, avoiding most of it, but the man looked as if he'd just stepped out of a shower.

Alison watched as Beka giggled and then squealed as the man—Death? And just what kind of a name was that anyway—whirled around and caught her close to him. "There, now you can get as wet as I am," he taunted. Beka pulled away from him with another laugh and walked to the edge of the spring where Smokie was drinking vast quantities of water.

"So what is this place? I've been to Sunshine Trails several times but never this area. It's lovely, but I don't see why we're here," she said.

"It's a wishing spring. I know it's a little out of the way, but it's a perfect addition to Sunshine Trails. It's not like we have anyplace else in this dimension where there is a true night and day. We'd all look like the walking dead if we didn't spend a little time in the park getting a bit of sunshine. Anyway, I wanted you to see it under the full moon and make a wish. Throw in a coin." Death walked over to stand behind her.

Beka dug into a pocket of her jeans and pulled out something. Alison leaned forward in expectation, hoping it was a penny. It was. She watched the girl close her eyes and then toss the penny into the air. A small splash signaled its entry into the water and, inside Alison, one more rope chaining her to the spring loosened. *"One more to go,"* that voice inside her head whispered. Hope grew. One day her curse would be finished, and she would be free of the confines of the spring. She looked over her shoulder toward the weeping willow. It wasn't going to be as easy for Cassia and not knowing how to help her made Alison sad. An aggravated voice had her turn back to the action on the other side.

"Smokie! Get off me, you furry, wet ape. This is not what I wished for. Who wants to kiss a Hellhound? Gross, Hellhound spit. Yuck."

"Oh?" Death leaned over and pushed Smokie off Beka. "Were you hoping for a kiss from someone else?"

"You know I can't tell you what I wished for, silly, or it won't come true."

Alison watched. The scene seemed to stand still in time for her for a second with Death leaning over Beka as she gazed up at him. Alison gave a long sigh at the romantic scene. Slowly, Death reached out and took both of Beka's hands in his and drew her up so she was standing next to him.

He is quite dashing, Alison thought, *with his dark hair tied back and a five o'clock shadow outlining his strong jaw.* He looked like a movie actor Alison had seen once in an old-fashioned Hollywood magazine. She turned her attention to Beka. She was…short. Somehow with her voice, Alison had expected someone taller, but Beka was…short. Smokie stood next to the couple and while he only reached to Death's waist, he stood almost as tall as Beka's chest. She was the girl-next-door cute and slender with long, dark wavy hair half way down her back. She was clad in faded jeans and a white, man's button-down shirt. Alison drew in her breath when she saw the boots though. They looked like leather and had an array of buckles and straps along the shaft that ran up to mid calf. It had been years since she could wear boots. Sometimes, she thought, the lack of a shopping spree was the hardest part to bear about her curse. Heck, she'd even settle for window-shopping at this point. *"Girl,"* the voice inside her head said, *"do you have any idea how many times you have thought about shoes over the past twe—"*

"Hush," she interrupted. *"Never stand between a girl and a pair of shoes."* The chuckle echoed a bit through her head, but there were no further comments. *For now.*

The couple hadn't moved. They were too busy looking at each other. *Yeesh, kiss her,* Alison thought. *Kiss her.* Death towered over Beka's slim form, and then he bent his head and kissed her. Alison breathed a sigh of relief.

Death and Beka broke apart and he wrapped his arms around her, holding her tight against him. Alison felt like a peeping Tom, but really there was so little to do around here and it was nice to see two people who fit together so well.

She sat daydreaming a little—or was it moondreaming? She giggled to herself. The hope inside her felt warm and happy, and she basked in that feeling for a moment. Maybe someday she'd find someone like Beka seemed to have. A yip from Smokie drew her out of her reverie. She opened her eyes to find herself looking across the pond and straight into Death's gaze. He still held Beka close, but now his head was raised and he was staring at…her? Looking at…her? No one had been able to look at her for almost twenty years. How was that possible? Alison drew in a deep breath. Wait. The Hellhound. Smokie. He had seen her as well and had touched her. A wink from Death held her spellbound.

"One more to go," he said loud enough for her to hear. "And, it will be soon. Then you have a little job to do for Thomas." Alison didn't know what he was talking about, but somewhere inside herself she knew he was right and there was a job she had to do when she was free. She nodded.

"What are you talking about? Who are you talking to?" Beka asked, pulling her arms from around Death's neck and stepping back.

"Nothing to worry about. Just a little errand for Thomas."

"You are not his messenger boy. Why didn't he do it? Is that why we're here at 4 a.m.?"

"He doesn't like to come down here. Something to do with the water mist and his feathers. Plus, he needed one more penny. Seemed he miscounted visitors. Silly Angel never was very good at math. Come on. Let's go to the Shadow Street Diner. I'm in the mood for the world's best pancakes."

At the word pancakes, some serious woofing came from the underbrush and Alison could hear Smokie crashing his way back.

Alison heard Beka giggle. With a last glance and a nod at Alison, Death threaded his fingers through Beka's, and they began to walk down the path. Smokie bolted out from the shrubs and onto the path. He stopped for a second and looked toward Alison, those blue eyes glowing in the shadows. A soft *chuff* and he was gone.

"Silly Angel, my ass!" the voice inside her sounded indignant before he cut himself off and fell silent, leaving Alison to ponder for a moment just who that voice belonged to. She shrugged and looked over at the willow. There was no noise, not even a ripple from beneath its lacey boughs. She lowered herself into the water and swam to join Cassia. It was dark, but enough light filtered in through the branches to let Alison see Cassia's hunched body on the bank. The Oceanid had her face buried in her hands and her slight body shook as sobs wracked her body. Alison swam quickly to her side and pulled herself out of the water to sit next to Cassia. Alison wrapped her arms around the Oceanid and held her gently, making soothing noises.

"We'll figure something out, Cassia. I promise I won't stop until I can help you, too. There has to be a way out of your situation. We'll find it."

Soft hiccupping sounds escaped from Cassia. She seemed to be trying to control her tears but not doing a good job of it from Alison's perspective. And who could blame her? Alison's curse was only a few decades old—Cassia's was almost a thousand years. Tears stung Alison's eyes when she thought of how lonely and hopeless Cassia must have felt year after year of being tied to this spring, waiting for her one true love to find her and knowing he never could.

She remembered the look in Cassia's eyes when she had finally told Alison her story. That look of utter despair. What had been sadder was the love that had still shone, regardless of what a twit her love had been. Going off to rescue some silly dragon. Then disappearing, probably eaten up by the very dragon he had gone to save. Alison wished she could go punch him for Cassia, but that wasn't an option. He was long gone, and Cassia's curse had no chance of being lifted.

"You've been so good to me, Alison," Cassia whispered. "I don't know why you ever forgave me for what I did to you. I only hope someone can help you soon."

"*Shhh*, Cass, it's okay. I'm glad it happened, honestly. It's given me a chance to appreciate things fully. Stop upsetting yourself." Alison hugged Cassia tight, and together they rocked back and forth until the moon began to set and the sun's rays began to paint the sky a faint yellow.

Alison drew Cassia to her feet, and they walked over to the small cave they called home. After tucking Cassia into her bed of soft leaves and grasses, she went to her own little nest and fell into an exhausted sleep. But the dreams came...

Twenty years ago...

"Here it is. See I told you. Look at all those coins. We can take enough to go to the movies and even get some popcorn." Emma's shrill voice caused Alison to wince. She looked at the spring and saw coins sitting on the silt under the clear waters. There must have been hundreds. Far from being tempted to gather them like her sister, she wanted them to stay. Each coin represented a wish from its thrower—a hope, a dream. They weren't there for movie tickets or popcorn. Emma was now up to her knees in the water, bending over time and again to gather more and more coins.

"Stop it, Emma. That money isn't yours. It belongs to the spring. You shouldn't take it. Come on, we'll ask Mom for a few dollars. That's all we need. This summer after graduation, we can get jobs and go see all the movies we want." Alison reached over, grabbed her sister's arm, and tried to guide her toward the bank. Emma angrily pulled her arm away and bent again.

Out of the corner of her eye, Alison caught a shadow and turned to look. Her eyes widened at what she saw. Treading water in the middle of the spring was a young lady. Long black hair trailed behind her and her penetrating blue gaze was fixed on Emma and Alison. The expression on her face was far from friendly or welcoming.

"Um…Emma, get out now. Look. Look over there. Someone is watching us."

Emma didn't look, instead concentrating on stuffing more and more coins in her pockets. "Just shut up, you brat, and help me. I've done this before, and no one has ever been here. It's in the middle of nowhere."

"You've stolen coins from here before?" Alison was sad, and she stopped worrying about the woman in the spring for a moment. This wasn't how their mother had raised them. Their father had died in a car accident years before, and their mom was barely able to support them on her salary from the grocery store, but she always had taught them that earning what they needed was the only way.

"It's not stealing. It's no one's money, and I need it more than the water does."

"Actually, girl, it's my money, and you are taking what is mine." The low-pitched voice grew louder as the woman swam behind Emma.

Emma twirled, her mouth agape as she realized there really was someone watching them.

Now she believes me, Alison thought.

"Wh-who are you?" Emma stuttered. Alison had never seen her at a loss for words before. Usually Emma brazened it out in bad situations, and, boy oh boy, had there been situations. Too many for Alison to count, but never one this serious...or strange.

"I am the guardian of this spring, and you are taking away wishes and dreams. Wishes and dreams that have no hope of ever coming true, now. Put them down and leave. Never come back here." The woman's eyes grew stormier with each word, and Alison could swear she felt her hair starting to stand on end as tingles raced along her skin. She shivered in growing fear and grabbed Emma's arm again, tugging and pulling it.

"That's stupid," Emma said. "These are just coins. Coins here for the taking. They belong to no one, not you, not the spring. They're mine." She ran the flat of her free hand along the surface of the water, sending a spray of water at the woman. "Go away and leave me alone."

Alison's tugging on Emma's arm finally had some effect, and Emma went off balance. She had to grab onto Alison for support to stop from falling.

"You think you are so smart, little girl? I don't think so. I think you need to learn a lesson. Listen to my words. You are destined to remain at the spring with me to understand the error of your ways. You will stay until a hundred dollars in pennies have been thrown into the waters and a wish is made for you." The guardian reached up to grab Emma, but Emma stepped back and pushed Alison into the guardian's grasp.

"No!" Both Alison and the guardian cried out at the same time, but it was too late. Like a rope being drawn tight, Alison felt the weight of the enchantment wrap around her body and what sounded like a lightning bolt sizzled through the air. *"It is done,"* a voice whispered in her head.

Emma splashed her way to the bank and stood there, her eyes wild and scared. Then, suddenly, she started to laugh. She pointed at Alison who stood there frozen, still held by the guardian.

"Look at the two of you. You both deserve each other. Stick-in-the-mud goody-two-shoes. No one helps anyone. You have to help yourself. I'm going to the movies, and I'm getting lots of popcorn." She jingled the coins in her pocket and ran down the path.

"Nooooo. Emma, don't leave me here. Please, come back." Alison pulled herself out of the guardian's arms and following Emma's example splashed her way to the edge. She climbed to the bank and started to follow Emma, but something stopped her. It was like she slammed into an invisible wall. She couldn't go any further.

She looked over her shoulder and saw the guardian treading water, a sad look on her face. "I'm sorry," the woman said. "It was supposed to be her, not you. But when I touched you, the curse fell on you. I'm so sorry."

Alison fell to her knees on the soft grassy bank and began to weep. She heard the woman say something above her, but a voice in her head spoke, *"One thousand pennies to go."* She moaned as the roaring in her ears increased until everything was drowned out. The tears didn't stop even when she felt the woman's arms enfold her, and she was held tight.

Present day…

"Alison. Alison, wake up. It's just a dream, honey. It's just a dream."

Alison woke to the dim glow lighting the little cave and Cassia's concerned face.

"I'm okay, Cassia. I'm okay." Alison sat up and wrapped her arms around her drawn knees. "Somehow, someday, we're both going to be free. I can't believe there is nothing to free you."

"There isn't, honey. You know my chance of freedom disappeared when my love died. I will be tied to this spring forever or until it dries up and I fade with it."

"Cassia, I remembered something from my dream. When you came to me on the bank that first day, you said something. What did you say?"

Alison saw a bit of confusion on Cassia's face as the Oceanid thought and then a flicker of a smile as she seemed to remember. "I wished your sister a very long life full of youth. I could think of no other wish for one such as she."

"How is that bad?" Alison questioned.

"Your sister probably would not think so either, but I am a believer of circles. You've probably heard it as you reap what you sow. I wanted to make sure she had the opportunity to reap what she'd sown."

Alison thought about that for a moment then looked at Cassia and laughed. For the first time in a long time, Cassia laughed back.

"It will work out, Cassia. It's just one more penny and I'm free, right?"

"Well…it's not quite that simple. The person who throws it in has to make a wish for you—and there's a catch, they can't be told to wish for you."

"What? But how is that going to work? And…and what if it doesn't happen? What happens next? The possibility of that happening must be close to impossible." Alison could almost feel her heart sink to her feet as despair washed over her.

"Then it starts all over again. Don't worry, Alison. Something tells me it's going to work out. Just wait and see." Cassia patted Alison's shoulder and turned and left her sitting in the cave, too stunned to say a word.

One more penny…

"Let it go, Emma. I'm tired of talking about it with you. I've wanted to see what this path leads to for a long time now and you keep stopping me. What's going on? I told you a month ago we were through. You just don't get it. We have nothing in common and I want you to stop following me and showing up wherever I go. What do I need to do to make you understand that?" The young man's voice was tight with anger and his low baritone had no problem reaching Alison's ears. At the sound of the next voice, she sat up straight in shock. *No, it can't be*, she thought. *Not after all these years.*

"I don't want to walk down that way, Deacon. There are too many tangles and thorns. Let's go back and follow the other path. It's cleaner, and my heels won't get caught in the stones. Besides, I want to talk to you about everything. I miss you." The voice was shrill and petulant.

It's Emma, Alison thought. *It's really her.*

"Stop, Deacon. I swear I won't go one more step."

"Fine, go back. I didn't want you following me anyway."

"Fine yourself. There is nothing down there but a stupid, old spring. Have fun. I'm going to go find my fun somewhere else."

"How does she know there is a spring down here?" Alison heard him ask out loud as he approached the bank. "Why am I even wondering? Good riddance."

Alison's anticipation grew as Deacon got closer. His deep voice did something inside her that no one else's ever had. It actually felt like little fish were inside her tummy swimming around and bumping into each other. When he stepped into view, she gasped. He was dreamy.

"Dreamy?" the voice asked. *"No one uses that word anymore. You're supposed to use something like hunk or hot or handsome or—"*

"Did you swallow a thesaurus that only had words that start with H?" she interrupted. *"Don't you have something better to do?"*

"Not really. I'm rather enjoying the show, or rather, the preview."

"Huh?"

"Never mind."

Alison stopped listening to her inner visitor and watched as Deacon sat on the grass. He stared at the rocks and the waterfall for a while before lying back, gazing at the sky. Alison looked up and saw the puffy white clouds chasing each other. They blocked the sunshine over and over again, racing their shadows across the ground. His eyes kept closing for longer and longer periods of time until he slept.

Alison couldn't help herself. She finally swam to the bank, careful not to make a sound. She stood and waded out of the warm water to the grass, tippy toeing over to simply stare down at him. There was something about Deacon that drew her. She didn't know what, but she had never felt like this before—excited, anxious, sad—all the emotions rolled over and through her like the clouds above.

She sat next to him, knowing that even if he woke, he couldn't see her. His lashes lay long and thick against his skin. *Why do men always have the nicest eyelashes? It's totally unfair.*

"Here we go again," the voice said, sounding resigned. *"Can't we talk about something else?"*

"I really can't discuss current events, you know." Alison sighed. *"It's been awhile since that newspaper page blew in here and even then it was just the classifieds."*

She continued to gaze at Deacon, memorizing his details, wanting to impress his image in her thoughts to keep safe. Not for the first time she despaired her fate, but for this one moment in time, he was hers.

"Young love is so painful to watch," the voice whispered in her head. *"I remember a long time ago there was this other water nymph who fell in love with someone who just watched himself in the water. He fell in love with his own reflection and had no time for her. That one didn't turn out very well."*

"You're talking about Echo and Narcissus?" Alison asked. *"Just how old are you? You must be ancient."*

"Enough of that. Age is only a number you know. After all, you are over thir—"

"Look at that squirrel," Alison interrupted the voice. *"Isn't he just adorable?"*

"Yes, let's change the subject. For now. I'll be back. I have to run a short errand." A chuckle went through her head and then the voice went silent.

"And stay away," she muttered.

The next few hours passed quickly. Alison sat guard over Deacon, from what she didn't know, but it made her feel needed chasing away a few curious spiders. While she couldn't interact with them like Cassie could, she could send little bursts of static electricity towards them and change their direction. Deacon slept on, and she hoped she had a little more time with him before he woke and left.

"I'm back. Did you miss me?

"Um…no, not really. Don't you have more errands you could run for a while?"

"You shouldn't just sit here gawking, girl. You know I haven't heard you sing for a while. Why don't you sing something?"

"Last time I sang you said I was off-key and to stop the caterwauling."

"Sing something pretty. I'm in a mood."

Alison sighed. *"Okay."*

Alison looked at Deacon. She knew immediately which song she would sing for him. She'd heard it enough times from Cassia when she was mourning the loss of her love. Cassia's songs were not like what Alison had known. The song made her think of knights and unicorns and fairy tales. She began to sing in her soft contralto.

I once was in a distant land
And far away at that same time
In a place so different yet
You stood and watched the suns shine down
And wondered even then

Through space and time
Through fate or chance or even destiny
A day arose when stars aligned
And separate pieces met

I stood beside the fields of grass
Within a forest green
I turned to look and there beheld
My true love on the path

All through the light and shadows dark,
We'll keep our love so true
We'll walk the paths that life brings
And smell the wildflowers.

The sun shines brighter now
The stars burn hotter too
Everyday feels like the first
For now we are together.

Deacon felt himself gradually awaken to the soft tones of someone singing a haunting melody. He stayed still and didn't open his eyes. *She must be sitting right next to me*, he thought. *It's lovely, but how strange.* It was like an old-fashioned song that made him think of the tales of Camelot, dragons, and Arthur that he had learned in inter-dimensional history. When the singer paused, he opened his eyes and looked. No one was there, but the song's words continued to ring through his head for a moment.

"Who is there? Where are you?" he asked. "I can hear you. Come out and show yourself."

His ears were met with dead silence—even the crickets stopped their humming.

"Please, I didn't mean to be so abrupt," he pleaded as he sat up. "Your song is lovely. I want to hear it again." He heard a slight rustle to his side and turned to look, but no one was there.

"Y-you can hear me?" a girl's voice whispered. "Y-you can really hear me?"

"Where are you? I can't see you," he replied.

"I'm right here, next to you. No one has been able to hear me for years. I don't understand why…"

"Who are you? What…are you?" Deacon wondered for a moment if he was dreaming, but the warm breeze on his face and the furtive rustling in the underbrush proved he wasn't.

"My name is Alison. I'm a…well…I'm one of the guardians of this spring."

For the next few hours they talked. Deacon wanted to learn everything about her, her likes, her dislikes. She seemed to soak up all the latest news about what had happened in the world since she'd been tied to the spring. In turn, he told her about himself, his travels, his studies.

As dusk drew near, he knew something special was happening between them. He wondered how this could work—if it could work—but for this moment he didn't care. All that was important was to talk to Alison, to hear her voice, to be close to her. Tomorrow would take care of itself. Still, he had to try and find out more.

"How can you leave this spring? Is there a way the curse can be broken?" he asked.

"There are several things that must happen, but I can't talk about them. They will either happen or not. It's not up to me."

"What do we do until then? I want to talk to you again. I'll come back, but truthfully I don't want to leave."

"It's okay," Alison whispered. "I'll still be here tomorrow and the day after that and the day after—"

"Shh, trust me, Alison. I'll be back. I promise."

A few more parting words and Deacon left.

Alison watched him. He never looked back but walked steadfastly down the path until he disappeared in the growing gloom of night. She stifled a sob. He was gone. It had been the most perfect afternoon ever but now would she ever see him again? She could only pray he would return. That night, she tossed and turned, dozing but never falling into a deep sleep.

She was up and out of the cave's entrance at first light going to the bank and finding a soft spot she could sit and wait—a spot that was the closest she could get to the barrier to see Deacon take that first turn around the bend in the path.

Hours passed and still no sign of Deacon. Cassia swam over several times, her face troubled. Alison waved her off each time. She didn't want to talk, not to Cassie and not to the aggravating visitor in her head who had thankfully remained silent today thus far.

The midday sunshine burned down upon her when she finally gave up. She stood and walked to the water's edge.

...We'll walk the paths that life brings
And smell the wildflowers.

The sun shines brighter now—

She squealed in joy, interrupting the singer. *"Ouch, girl,"* her inner visitor's voice held a wince, but she ignored it. All she cared about was getting to the barrier to see Deacon.

"You came back."

"I'm sorry, Alison. I wanted to be here sooner, but I had a flat tire and for some reason my spare was flat, too. I didn't mean to worry you. I'm here now. And this is the only place I want to be. I thought about our talk all night and couldn't wait to get here."

She moved as close to him as she could, and, for the moment it was enough.

Every day during the next week, Alison woke at first light and hurried to get ready. She spent hours combing her hair, checking her reflection in the spring, straightening and smoothing out her only dress. *Spring nymphs have the ugliest dresses,* she grumped to herself. Why couldn't they be blue or violet instead of green? A long suffering sigh echoed through her head. She giggled. *"No, really. We just fade into the grasses and leaves."*

"Girl, that's enough. Boots, dresses, hair. We have to get you something else to think about."

"I could think about Deacon."

"Arrghhh. That's it. I have something else to take care of. Behave yourself."

She swam to the reeds and waited for Deacon to start down the path. *This is stupid. I get ready for him, and he can't even see me. I don't know why I'm doing this.* But deep inside she did. She was madly, hopelessly in love with Deacon. *It doesn't matter I've only known him for a week. It seems like forever.*

Her thoughts were interrupted hearing Deacon's familiar singing as he approached, and she went to meet him.

"Hi, Deacon."

"Hi, sweetie. I never thought I'd get here today. One thing after another and a small argument with this stupid girl—"

"So here you are. And look who you are with. Poor Alison, still trapped to this stupid old spring. I should have known you two would be sneaking around behind my back."

"Why are you here, Emma," Deacon asked, "and how do you know Alison? Can you see her?"

"Of course I can see her. Can't you? Ha, you can't, can you? How sad. What a stupid look on your face, Alison. Are you in love with him? Well, we all know how this will work out, don't we?"

"Well, hello to you, too. Deacon, this is my sister. I haven't wanted to talk about her during our conversations and bring us both down. So, Emma, you finally came back to say hello to me and Cassia."

"As if. I came because I heard in town that Deacon was spending a lot of time on walks. I just knew I'd find him here. Look at the two of you. How pathetic." Emma tossed her blond hair back and strode up to Deacon. She pushed against his chest and shoved him back away from Alison. Over and over again she pushed, continually screaming invectives at him, driving him to the edge of the bank. He threw his arms out in an effort to stabilize himself, but it was too late. With one last push, he went off-balance and started to fall.

"I wish you would change places with your sister," he cried out as he was tossed backward into the spring.

Snap.

Alison felt the last strand break inside her. The air rippled around her and a loud *crack* rent the air, its echo sounding like thunder. *"The last penny,"* that little voice whispered. *"You're free, but please remember, you have one last task."*

Alison threw her arms in the air and laughed then hugged herself. She looked at Deacon. He sat, up to his neck in the water, a confused look on his face that was gradually replaced by one of happiness.

She laughed again in joy as he got up and waded over to her. She ran into the water and met him half way. She stared at him as he began to comprehend what had happened.

"I can see you, Alison. I can really see you. You're beautiful. Is it over?" He tentatively reached out one hand, drew it back and then, finally, reached for a strand of hair that hung over the side of her face and brushed it away from her eyes.

"It's over. I'm free to go." Alison could see her smile reflected in his face as he looked down at her.

He placed both hands on her shoulders and squeezed, as if making sure she was really there. With a whoop of pure joy, he grabbed her around her waist, lifted her high and twirled, their movements causing ripples to spiral out from where they stood. She looked down, caught in the moment of being able to touch him as well. She drew her hands over his hair and head and leaned forward as he pulled her nearer. She slid down against his body and then, they kissed for the first time.

"Worth the wait?" the little voice whispered.

"Get out and stay out," she ordered back. She distinctly heard a chuckle in her mind, and then forgot everything as she became lost in Deacon's kiss. She reluctantly came back to the present as she heard Emma's shriek of disbelief. Pulling back, she looked at the bank where Emma and Cassia stood, face to face. She watched as Emma put both arms out and pushed Cassia back.

"No. No. No. I'm not staying here. You can't make me." Emma turned and began to jog along the grass.

Crash.

She came to a dead stop and fell backward onto the ground. With a howl, she jumped up, moved forward, and was stopped dead again at an invisible barrier. A barrier Alison was all too familiar with.

"I'm sorry, Emma, but you will have to stay here and this time the enchantment is on the person it should have been attached to all along. Don't worry, you and I will learn to get along." Cassia's tone belied her words and for a second Alison sensed the shred of doubt in her friend.

"But that's not fair," Emma said in her usual snippy tone. "He didn't throw in a penny when he made that wish."

"Actually, he was thrown in and if you check his pocket, he has exactly one penny in it." Cassia smiled and brushed a wet lock of hair from Emma's forehead. "I'm afraid you'll be here for a few years until a hundred dollars in pennies is collected and someone wishes you out. But don't worry, honey, we'll put the time to good use."

Alison watched as Emma began to jerk back from Cassia's touch and then hesitated. Emma gazed at Deacon and Alison. Emma closed her eyes and then opened them and stared straight at Alison. Comprehension seemed to finally dawn in Emma's face. For the first time that Alison could remember, a tear seeped from Emma's eye and trickled down her cheek.

"I didn't understand, Alison. I'm sorry."

"It's okay, Emma. Everything is going to be all right."

They threw themselves into each other's arms and hugged. They sat on the grass, and Cassia and Deacon moved away to give them some privacy. The girls spoke for several minutes before Alison asked Emma the question that had been haunting her every day over the years.

"Do you know where Mom is? Is she still alive? Did she ever know what happened?"

"The last time I saw her was about ten years ago. She was working at the Shadow Street Grocery Store and had an apartment around there. I haven't been back since." Emma looked down and at least had the grace to look abashed.

"It's okay, Emma. I'll find her and bring her back to visit, okay?"

Emma started to cry and dove into Alison's open arms, sobbing as if her heart would break. Cassia and Deacon came back and together they helped both girls to stand. Cassia kept her arm around Emma's shoulders and Alison saw an air of calmness descend over Emma.

"As for the two of you." Cassia turned her attention to Deacon and Alison. "You may not understand the full ramifications of what just happened. Remember, the enchantment changed places. Alison, you now have eternal youth, and I can extend it to Deacon. But we can talk about this later. For now, go and just be happy. You know where we are."

The enormity of what Cassia said washed over Alison and a quick look at Deacon showed her he didn't fully comprehend what had just happened. "We'll worry about that later, Cassia. Thank you."

Deacon drew Alison into his arms. "Let's go for a while. We will be back, Cassia, I promise."

Alison nodded and kissed both Cassia and Emma before turning to wait for Deacon. He hesitated a moment and awkwardly patted Emma on the shoulder, and with what looked like relief, turned away. A quick kiss on Cassia's cheek and he was back by her side, wrapping his hand around hers.

"Deacon, you have a car right?" Alison asked. "I have a little trip we have to make before this is all over. It will mean driving to the Shadow Street Grocery Store."

"Why in the world do you want to go over there?"

"I need to see if my mother is still alive. Also, I have it on good authority that the world's best pancakes are to be found at the diner. Do you have any idea how long it's been since I have had pancakes?"

Deacon laughed. "Then pancakes it is. Let's go."

Alison pushed back her empty plate. Not a scrap of chocolate chip pancakes remained. For a moment she seriously considered ordering another stack, but thought that two orders had been plenty. For now. "Those were definitely the best pancakes I've ever eaten, and I don't think it's because I haven't had them in such a long time. I have to admit though, I'm a little worried about our server. She's like a witch or something. I don't remember this diner being here before. A lot of things have changed."

Deacon finished chewing his last mouthful before responding. "Well, at the rate you inhaled them, I would bet you haven't eaten anything in a long time. Didn't you eat while you were there?"

"No, we didn't have to. I tried explaining chocolate to Cassia, but she had never eaten any. Can you imagine living for a millennia without ever once tasting it? I'm going to eat chocolate every day of the year."

"You'll get a fat ass, silly. Cass gave you eternal youth, not eternal-being-skinny."

"Oh, you're right. I may have to go ask her for an add-on." Alison giggled. "I wish the grocery store had known where Mom went. Still, it's a good lead that they have seen her walking around downtown once or twice. Do you think we should try going to the PI they recommended? He sounds a bit odd."

Deacon paused while counting money for the bill and looked up at her. "After what we've been through, please define odd."

"Um…right. Let's go."

Alison looked at the sign on the private investigator's door. "No Zenocanths?" she questioned. "What in the world is a zenocanth?"

"I think it's a big bug," Deacon responded.

"Actually," a deep voice sounded over their shoulders, "that is left over from the previous owner of this place. He ran a private investigation and dating agency out of this place."

Alison turned around. In front of her was the tallest person she'd ever seen. He even towered over Deacon.

For some reason the thought of Viking ships and old stone ruins came to her mind when she looked at him. That part of Earth's history had fascinated her during school. She had such a lot to catch up on.

"Um…and why would he need to specify no zenocanths? How many would just walk in from the street?"

"You'd be surprised. The last one that did was the reason he sold this business to me. I dropped the dating agency though. Do you have any idea how hard it is to work with some clients? I mean take vampires for instance. Everyone knows the half-dead can't be videotaped for the dating interview. Issues of filming aside, vampires need to lighten up and stop being so…well…dead."

Rather than thinking he was weird, Alison was enthralled. For some reason, she believed every word he spoke. There was something about him that made her trust him. Kind of like Cassia, she thought.

She laughed and held out her hand. "I'm Alison, and this is Deacon. I'm here to see if you can help me find my mother. I've been gone for quite some time. The Shadow Street Diner said you might be able to help us find her. Her name is Amy Raines."

"Well, this is an easy case. I won't even charge you. Come on in. I'm Niklaus by the way." She walked in behind him and noticed an older woman at the desk.

"I don't understand—Mom." Alison ran to the older woman sitting behind the reception desk.

"Alison? Alison? My darling girl, I've waited for you to come back for so long. I never gave up looking for you."

Alison and her mother laughed and cried and hugged, oblivious to the two men standing by the front door.

Alison stood at the sink in her mother's apartment. The afternoon and evening had been spent catching up with her mother and explaining everything that happened. Considering the very existence of Shadow Street, her mother had taken in everything and believed it. In turn, her mother told her some of the things she had seen with Niklaus' business.

"This is tame compared to some of the things we've had," her mother had told her. "Just last week we had a case that involved issues at the Moonlight Market. It seems there is a Hellhound that lives around here with a penchant for chocolate and sweets. Oh, the trouble that one was."

Alison looked at her mother. "The Hellhound's name wasn't Smokie, was it?"

"As a matter of fact—"

They had both giggled over that one. Alison rinsed another glass and put it in the strainer, then grew still. Her mother was in the dining room clearing off the table and humming a tune. A tune Alison knew all too well. Suddenly, she knew what her last task was.

"What's that song you're singing, Mother? Where did you hear it?"

"Niklaus sings it all the time. He said it was something his lost love used to sing to him. I feel so sorry for him. He truly mourns her."

"Mother! Deacon! Hurry before it gets dark. We need to get Niklaus."

Without a question, her mother grabbed her purse and Deacon his car keys. They raced to Niklaus' tall Victorian house at the outskirts of town.

Alison raced along the path, pulling Niklaus by the hand. She ignored his protests and only urged him to move faster. "Hurry, hurry. I promise you, you need to see this."

"All right. All right. I'm hurrying. What is it—Cassia? Cassia is that you?"

Alison stood and watched as Cassia stopped brushing her hair in mid-stroke and went still. She turned and when she saw who stood before her, the brush went to the ground as Cassia went into Niklaus' embrace.

Snap.

With that sound, Alison knew her last task was completed. She smiled when she heard the voice in her head once again.

"Thank you, little one, for honoring my last request."

"You seem to know and be able to do anything. Why didn't you bring Niklaus and Cassia together sooner? They have had so much pain and sorrow. She thought he was dead, and he thought she was as well."

"I'm an observer, a muse, a helper. If I went and changed everything to be perfect, what good is living? We all have to learn and grow and sometimes part of a life is to teach others. I try to right a few wrongs here and there when I am able. This is one of those times. Go and be happy."

"Goodbye."

"Oh, I didn't say goodbye, now did I?" the inner voice chuckled. *"We'll meet again."*

Alison giggled and looked up. Cassia and Niklaus still held each other tightly. Alison knew the Oceanid's curse was lifted and now she could be with her one true love. Emma stood to the side, hugging her mother. Both looked happy.

And as for her... Deacon stood on the bank waiting patiently. He smiled and held out his hand. She ran over to him and, together, they walked up the path with the sweet smell of wildflowers on the breeze.

One thousand pennies to go...

"Oooh, a wishing spring," the girl's voice said. "Do you have a penny?"

"Sure, honey. Here you go," a male voice responded. "Make a good wish."

Kerplunk.

"Nine hundred and ninety-nine more to go," a little voice whispered in Emma's head.

"Who are you?" she asked.

"Let's just say you and I are going to be good friends. I have a lot of things to teach you, but first I have to tell you about this couple I know and their Hellhound, Smokie. Have you ever seen what happens when you feed peanut butter to a Hellhound?"

She smiled, content to sit back and listen to the story, and wait.

LISOVYCK
The Shore
by Morgan Ashe

"Well at least this is better than the four a.m. walk you took me on weeks ago. What are we doing tonight? Is there another angry goddess on the loose? Do you need to go to Hell with Thomas like the two of you have been hinting? I really need to go find shoes for the prom. Two more weeks to go. Do I really have to go? I don't think I would miss much if we didn't go."

"Do you think you could slow your mouth for about five minutes? You're driving me insane with the constant chatter. This is so unlike you. What's going on?" Death sounded both exasperated and caring as he picked his way along the steep, rocky trail behind me.

I knew I had been talking a mile a minute since we met at the top of the trail, but how do you tell your prom date you can't find a dress with only two weeks to go. Show me a demon or an evil spirit and I have no problem knowing what to do and how to remove it. Put me in front of a store and tell me to get a prom dress and the accessories and I have no clue. Not one bit of fashion-sense DNA is in my body. I usually chose my outfits by walking up to the store mannequins and pointing at them to the sales lady. Hey, it works. Don't knock it. This way everything matches and I don't have to stand around and have internal debates on color hues and textures.

About the only thing I knew was I needed a lot of pockets for my charms, salt, and other paraphernalia that lets me do my job with the Shadow Keepers. I had worked for them as a spiritbinder since I was thirteen, and now four, almost five years later, I still help keep the evil at bay that threatens the residents and visitors of Shadow Street.

"What a beautiful full moon, Beka. Slow down for a moment and let's enjoy the ambiance a little, shall we?"

I looked up at the softly glowing orb. No matter where I had travelled in this dimension, the Dusky Moon always looked closer here in Shadow Street. Ordinary physics didn't apply so why should anything else? It took my thoughts back to a month ago, during *The Death before Drinking Goat's Blood Incident*. It had been a full moon then, also. I remembered looking up into the cloudless night sky, the cold stone of the altar's rock at my back as I waited for the priest's steel blade to descend, my body unable to move or protect myself. The burst of raw energies above me had overloaded my senses, and I had felt myself sink closer and closer into that final darkness waiting for all of us eventually. The darkness that crouched in the shadows to… I shook my head to escape that particular memory. At least good things had happened during the incident. I had met Death.

Yeah, yeah, I'm sure he has a name but so far he hasn't told me what it is no matter how much I tease, threaten, or beg. I swear I am going to start calling him Archibald if he doesn't tell me what it is.

Sudden barking, squawking, and a flurry of wings stopped my musing. It could only mean one thing. No, not demons.

"Smokie. What are you doing?"

I went off the trail and behind a bush only to receive a face full of feathers. "Oh. My. God. How did you find chickens in the middle of a forest? Get away from there." These were not normal fowl, they were easily twice the size of an ordinary chicken. I watched as more took flight to escape him and settled into branches too high for him to reach. "Chickens can fly?" I asked out loud. "Who knew?"

Death chuckled behind me. "Never a dull moment with him around. Although I do have to say the *Peanut Butter Stuck to the Roof of a Hellhound's Mouth Incident* may be my favorite to date. Watching him roll around trying to get that off was hilarious."

"Sure, at the cost of a vase and a smashed figurine. If nothing else, it gave Thomas something to talk about for the last few weeks. Let's keep all new food experiments outside from now on shall we?"

The rustle of a candy bar's wrapper in my pocket drew Smokie's attention away from the mutant chickens. He wheeled and came over, his gaze fixated on my pocket. A little spittle of drool proceeded to leak from his gigantic mouth and as usual sizzled as it hit the ground. That hiss never failed to make me ponder Hellhound dynamics for a brief second. But now was not the time for that. "You can have it in a little bit, Smokie. I don't want to ruin your pre-dinner snack. Let's go see what Death is so anxious to show us."

I picked my way along the remainder of the trail and was happy to reach level ground below. The dirt gave way to a sandy beach. The soft lap of the waves and the hum of the cicadas filled the air with their gentle noises. If I didn't have my dress and shoes issue, it would have been a perfect June evening.

Smokie raced ahead and stood knee deep in the ocean. I could hear the steam's *woosh* as his heat evaporated the water. Great, another bath to get salt out of his fur.

Death walked up behind me and grabbed my hand. "Over here," he said. "I have a little surprise for you."

He led me over to a pile of wood within a circle of stones. Another stack of wood was set to the side and a cooler. A folded blanket on top completed the setup. Everything had an eerie luminescence from the moon's light.

"What's all this?" I asked. "It looks like some people left their beach gear."

Silence and then a long-suffering sigh.

"What?" I started to ask, and then the light bulb turned on. *Oops!* "Ohhh, how lovely and thoughtful of you. A picnic at…um…midnight. This will be fun."

Death pushed me aside and grabbed the blanket. He stood in front of me and looked down from his great height and shook his head. Even with a frustrated look on his face, those aquiline features never failed to send a shiver of appreciation down my spine. The moon had him half in its pale light and half in shadow. "I have got to get you out more often, Beka. All work and no play."

"Hey, you know I watch movies with Uncle Jasper on Friday nights. He's finally out of that bizarre foreign subtitle movie with hidden meanings stage and into some old Earth-dimension '50s Roger Corman B-movie stage. What's not fun about that? You should have been here when he discovered some stray signals coming from the third dimension. If people really look like that there, I'm not sure I'd ever want to visit."

Death bent down and gave me a kiss that managed to silence me and to curl my toes at the same time.

"Beeeeekkkkkaaaaa. Where are you? I know you're here."

Oh no, I moaned silently, *not Merrick. Not now. Actually, what was he doing up at this time of night?*

I turned to watch my fourteen-year-old cousin run towards us.

"Merrick. What are you doing here? You're supposed to be home and in bed. It's a school night."

"I followed you on my bike. It's not fair. I'm always left out of the fun stuff."

"Maybe it's because you are only fourteen and have what's known as a curfew? Do your parents know you are out here?" I pulled my cell phone out of my front pocket and started searching for their speed dial.

"Um…no. No, don't call them, please."

"No can do, silly. I'm always in enough trouble with adults without adding this to it. Don't worry, I'll smooth it over."

After a brief discussion with his sleepy and irritated parents, I managed to persuade them that a few hours hooky with a Hellhound and Death was actually an educational experience that would help him later in life. Yeah, I'm that good.

I shut down my cell phone and turned to look at Merrick. "You owe me one. That's gonna be at least two walks with Smokie after school next week." I tried to look stern, but I knew walking Smokie was one of Merrick's favorite things. Not everyone can say they know a Hellhound.

"Where is Smokie? I didn't see him."

"Probably irritating a few nocturnal creatures. He'll be back in a minute when he realizes where the food is."

"Food? Cool. I'm starving."

"It's midnight. How can you be starving?"

"Beka, he's a growing boy. Don't worry, there is more than enough. Here, spread this out." Death looked at Merrick with a grin. "As for you, we'll discuss interrupting plans at a later time. For now let's enjoy the food and atmosphere."

I took the blanket from Death and smoothed it out beside the campfire while he lit some kindling, and Merrick ran along the beach looking for whatever fourteen year olds find interesting.

Soon the crackling of the fire and the snapping of the sap heating and exploding added to the night's sounds. Despite the warm day, the evening had grown cool and I sat on the blanket, grateful for the heat of the fire. Death had picked the perfect spot. A fallen, half buried tree trunk, its bark long gone and its wood smooth from countless years of sand and water polishing, gave a resting spot for the two of us. We had the forest behind and the ocean and fire in front. Merrick sat with his back to the water, seemingly oblivious to the beauty. His attention was focused squarely on the hamper and the possibilities that lay therein. Like most teenagers, he and his stomach were always in search of a meal.

A crashing to our side heralded the return of the Hellhound. Smokie came prancing along the sand, a few feathers suspiciously hanging from his mouth and for a moment I worried how many of the fowl were left, but decided since they were a mutant variety, Smokie may have saved me some trouble in the future. He sprawled almost on the fire facing me, or my pocket rather. He ignored the scratching that Merrick provided, his attention, like Merrick's, concentrated on that next meal. I guess the mutant chickens weren't enough of a snack or he needed a sugar chaser to go with all that protein.

I feasted on cheese and crackers and veggies and dip, while the men folk dug into the protein portion of the meal. I understood the need for meat. However, I abstained. Too many nights of watching blood sucking vampires and parts falling off of zombies had changed my dietary habits a bit. No, not on the television…in real life. Lately, even the tomato sauce on pasta made me queasy. Death and Merrick had no such qualms. Apparently years of seeing every possible method of death hadn't stopped Death from enjoying any and all forms of meat. He and Smokie shared a love for bacon and tonight was no exception.

I watched them wolf down what must have been two pounds of the crisp strips, awed that neither looked even half full when it was finished. Merrick, for his part, didn't care what form the food or calories came in and he ate so much, at one point I asked him how long the tapeworm had been living in his stomach. He just rolled his eyes at me and continued to stuff a strange mixture of crackers, cheese, bacon, and French onion dip into his mouth. At least he had the manners to keep it closed while chewing, but I shuddered at the combination.

"And now," Death said after putting away the remains of the meal, "it's time for the best part of the campfire. S'mores." He pulled out a plastic bag of graham crackers, some marshmallows, and another bag of chocolate squares. Smokie went on high alert, his body actually quivering. Merrick licked his lips.

"You think there's enough for seconds? I'm still hungry," he said.

I snorted as I looked at the crumbs on the front of his sweatshirt and the smear of French dip that graced the corner of his mouth. "I'm going to name that tapeworm if you don't stop feeding it."

"Aww, come on, Beka. You know the awesome deliciousness of s'mores. You can't stop at just one or two."

"I've never eaten a s'more."

"Excuse me?" Death gave me a look of disbelief. "Never?"

"Nope."

"I've said it before, Beka. You don't have enough fun in your life."

I watched while Death made me the first s'more, and I have to admit it was the most delicious thing I've eaten other than my favorite food, Ben & Jerry's Chunky Monkey. Entertainment for the evening began with Smokie eating several cooked marshmallows and getting that ooey gooey goodness stuck in the fur around his mouth. The cool ocean air semi-hardened the marshmallow, and he rolled around trying to remove it, which meant it now had sand mixed in. Somehow a few feathers got in there, too. He looked like a grunge version of Santa Hellhound. What a mess. It took a trip to the ocean for me to get it out, but it looked good enough until I could give him a bath. Merrick followed and managed to dowse everyone in so much salt water we looked like we'd been swimming all day.

I returned and collapsed next to Death.

"I swear I'm going to write a book on the care and feeding of Hellhounds. This past month I've learned more than anyone should have to know. *Hellhounds for Dummies.* Yeah, that's what I'm going to do."

"You love the furry beast, and you know it."

"Shhh, he'll hear you."

A soft *chuffing* at my side said it was too late, and I turned my head in time to get a full cheek lick from Smokie. "Eww, Hellhound spit," I complained, but couldn't stop myself from giving him a hug. He went back to the fire to lie down and soon steam started to rise from his drying fur. Merrick sat next to him, then stretched out, propping his head up with one hand and idly playing with Smokie's fur with the other.

Death yawned. His arms reached up in a huge stretch and, in a move that fooled no one, brought one arm down and around me. Smokie opened one blue, glowing eye and, apparently deciding that no sugar was involved, closed it again. Merrick just rolled his eyes and made *eww* sounds before his attention returned to whatever fourteen-year-old teens think about. I shuddered and stopped myself from further speculation. Rather than a smart-ass remark I decided to go with the flow and snuggle closer, leaning my head against Death's shoulder. The ocean view, a warm fire, the sound of Smokie's snoring, a fourteen-year-old semi-run away with an insatiable appetite, and Death. All in all, it was a perfect evening…er…early morning.

I chased the thoughts of prom dresses and shoes away for the moment. Tomorrow was another day.

"Things weren't always this peaceful on this spot, you know," Death said in a near whisper. "There was a time when an event began at the main wharf on First Street and continued on to the house on the hill here."

"What house?" I asked. "We didn't pass anything as we came here, and why are you whispering?"

"*Shhh*. If you look at the top of the ridge, you'll see what is left of the place—a stone chimney and foundation."

"There it is," Merrick said, pointing a finger. He spoke in the same hushed tones that Death had.

I turned and sure enough, silhouetted by the moon's light, a tall, thin structure stretched into the evening sky. I took Death's word that the foundation was there as well.

"What happened?"

"It was a dark and stormy night—"

I snorted. "Is this the scary story part of tonight's entertainment? Wasn't *The Marshmallow Stuck to a Hellhound's Fur Incident* enough?"

"Hush, you. This is part of the learning-to-have-more-fun portion."

"Fine, I'll hush. Tell me the spooky tale."

"It was a dark and stormy night…" Death began, again in that scary whisper and this time I let the sound of his voice take me into his tale.

The Perun

The citizen's of Shadow Street hadn't seen a storm of that magnitude for decades. The flashes of lightning went on and on, unceasing in their intensity and the accompanying thunder seemed to sound simultaneously with each bolt. Old-timers looked at the ceilings of their houses with a knowing look and hunkered down to weather it out. Others had never seen or heard such fury and prayed long into the night to whatever deity they believed in, praying for it to cease and for their families to survive to see another day.

It was the month of the Dusky Moon, and daylight would be around for a few hours. The morning dawned clear and quiet, belying the storm of a few hours before. Puffy clouds floated effortlessly in a gray sky while left over puddles on the cobblestone roads and walkways started to dry up. Even the ocean's waves were calm, gentle swells rippled and rolled the surface, only their muddied appearance giving evidence to the unrest of the night before.

Viktor checked the rigging on his fishing boat. The storm had left the deck a mess. "Hurry up, Seamus. We've missed an entire morning of fishing. I'd like to get out and at least make one net run before dusk," he said to the first mate.

"Aye, Cap'n," his mate said without looking up from his inspection of the nets. "The nets are lookin' good. Should'na be mor'n an hour or so."

Viktor heard shouting behind him and turned to see a group of people gathered at the end of the dock pointing out away from the town. He looked outward toward open waters and saw what had captured everyone's interest.

A ship, her sails torn and rent, and two of her masts broken was drifting from around the rocky point. She must have been a sight to behold before the damage...a whaler by the looks of her. He grabbed his telescope. It revealed even more damage. A quick look at the bow showed the name—*Perun*. His Russian was rusty, but he remembered the language from his younger days in Odessa before he and his family had escaped into the last portal. The myths of his forefathers had been taught to him at an early age at his parents' feet. It took only a moment to recall that Perun had been the god of thunder and lighting. An unusual name for a ship.

"Weigh the anchor, Seamus. We have something more important than fishing."

Within minutes the anchor was drawn, and they were underway. Viktor's fishing boat was small, but he hoped there was a rope or some method of getting up to the Perun's deck. Worst case would be to climb his ship's mast and swing over. Luck was with him, however, and several ropes from the rigging hung over the side.

He left Seamus on *The Rose* and proceeded to go aboard. A glance around showed that the destruction on the deck was more than what a storm could do. The heavy masts lay across the decks, splintered and crushed to pulp. Planks from the deck hadn't been broken, but rather burst from within. The sails hung, torn in ribbons from top to bottom as if caught up by the claws of some giant beast.

He quickly searched below deck. Hammocks were in disarray. Holes in the hull and floor showed signs of further destruction. He could not see what lay below this floor to the hold and was ashamed he was coward enough not to try. Viktor called out in case someone had survived, but not a sound or sign of life was present. It was a ghost ship.

The cold October air did nothing to reduce the chill of the crew's quarters as he climbed the stairs, and then walked cautiously around the main deck's debris, toward the bow. The try-works, where sailors rendered the blubber to whale oil was crushed, its bricks torn from their foundation and strewn about.

The bowsprit, which usually projected many feet in front of the hull, sagged, twisted and warped, caught in the ropes and rigging of the sails furled around its length, but the figurehead remained unscathed. He knew it was meant to embody the spirit of a ship. It was there to placate the sea gods and ensure a safe voyage to the sailors and passengers. This one had done neither, he thought. Half man, half goat, carved from the trunk of a giant oak, it was one of the few pieces of wood that hadn't been broken or split. Strange symbols were carved into the wood. Whatever had caused the damage here must not have been strong enough to cleave through its massive girth. It hung precariously from the iron spars and screws that were affixed into the hull. Its massive weight kept threatening to pull it down and into the ocean. Its existence however was not a matter of importance to him. He wanted to know what had caused this catastrophe.

A sudden banging startled him, and he whirled to see who—or what—had caused the noise. The door to the captain's quarters caught the wind again and crashed against the side. He moved to investigate the room. Like the rest of the ship it was torn asunder, mattress stuffing spilled out to the floor, linens torn and piled here and there, and every object in the room was either broken or tipped over. What stopped him cold and riveted his attention was the far wall. There, written in what looked like blood, still glistening and damp was a hastily scrawled word——Lisovyk. It couldn't be. They were just myths—the daydreams or nightmares of peasants. He wanted nothing more than to leave the ship and find the nearest church to cleanse his soul or bar to wash the anxiety away. Perhaps both.

After searching the room and finding the captain's logbook he spent precious moments reading the last entry, starting and stopping over and over again to glance around, certain that something or someone watched him. It felt as if the very air was getting heavier with the presence of something. Not some*one*, he thought. Some…*thing*.

The feeling lifted as the sound of excited voices drew him to the doorway. The voices grew louder and more excited as several sailors came on board. He went over to talk but stopped as they turned away to help others climb up the same rigging he had used minutes before. He looked over the water and saw a flotilla of boats either anchored near the hull or underway towards *The Perun* as the curious and the nosey hurried to see what had happened. Within minutes the deck was crowded with onlookers and officials, eager to see what had happened. He could tell by the avaricious glint in their eyes that the salvaging of the contents of the sailor's trunks as well as the hold would soon commence.

He tried to talk to the mayor and then the town council. One by one they turned away. No one wanted to hear what he had to say and his warnings fell on deaf ears. The fairytales of uneducated peasants held no interest to them, not when a windfall like this sailed in and there was no one to claim the wealth. No one wanted to hear any tales from Earth's history. After all, didn't they live with and see the unusual everyday? What more could this be?

He stood on the deck, the captain's log in his hand, uncertain of his next move. A loud groan halted all conversation. Another had everyone rushing to where the bowsprit dangled over the waters. The deck's fragile railing provided little for a barrier and the crushing mob sent a few people screaming over the edge and into the waters below. A moment later the sound of iron, weak from damage groaned again and the screws holding the massive weight of the figurehead to the hull gave way, snapping. The wooden goat-man plunged into the waters and disappeared beneath its azure waves. The resulting splash sent a spray of water up and over the onlookers, drenching them in its brine.

Viktor remained on his feet, the captain's log protected by his coat. For one moment he wondered about the pristine figurehead and then shook off his worries and made his way back to the stern. He climbed down the riggings to his boat where Seamus waited, patiently checking the fishing nets, unconcerned with the hubbub of the crowds above.

With *The Rose's* deck swaying back and forth with the motion of the waves, Victor stood, feet braced apart to keep his balance and looked once again at the damage of the ship.

"More storms a comin', Capt'n," Seamus said in that slow drawl of his. He looked up at Viktor and a silent understanding passed between the two men. Viktor nodded and turned. He began to weigh anchor and after a few moments, *The Rose* began its short journey back to the dock.

The next days were spent with townspeople arguing over rights to the wreckage and cargo. Viktor spoke out against using any of it. However, the mayor won and the *Perun* was taken apart plank by plank and hauled away to the top of the cliffs overlooking the ocean and the dock. Within a few days the ship was completely demolished and the structure of the mayor's two-story house began to tower above the rocks.

It didn't take long however for the rumors to start. It was hard to keep men working on the house. Those that did, toiling by lantern, began to speak in hushed tones of the strange goings on there. Whispers from corners, shadows moving on walls with nothing there to cast them. Fishermen reported wispy blue lights swirling like fog in the dark of night where the skeletal lines of the house stood. Several villagers who had taken wood from the abandoned ship spoke of voices in the night, calling to them. Sibilant hisses of hatred and death filled the dark areas of their homes. Bonfires were made from the wood and any other item from the *Perun*.

Except for the house on the hill.

The mayor was in denial. He publically railed against anyone that believed something supernatural was happening and insisted the work on his house continue, to no avail. Within a month, the workers abandoned the site and no one could be persuaded to continue despite all the pleas and threats from the mayor.

One evening, Viktor heard shouts and screams. He raced from *The Rose* to the dock and over to the town square where a crowd had gathered.

At the center of the melee, a woman, her cries of anguish rising above the clamor of the villagers, knelt over the body of a small child.

"The child was found at the construction site," one villager told Viktor. "She and her brother went out to play last night and never returned. We still haven't found the boy."

"No one knows what killed her," another one spoke. "Look at her face. She looks like she was scared to death."

Viktor took one look at the body and then turned and looked up the hill. In his heart he knew what he needed to do. Without a word, he left and returned to *The Rose* to gather a few things. Seamus helped him, his usual taciturn face even more emotionless than ever. He put a hand on Viktor's shoulder as Viktor started to step on the gangplank.

"I'll come with ye, Capt'n."

"No, I need you here, Seamus. If things work out as they must up there you have to keep the townsfolk away until the fire has died down. We can't risk more lives. I think once it starts, they will finally see reason and listen to you. If they don't, well…" Viktor held his hand out to Seamus and was met with a firm grasp. Putting aside his fears, he squared his shoulders and began the long walk to the deserted building site.

The farther out from the docks he walked, the quieter the sounds became. A chill formed deep inside him, and he shuddered as his imagination went into overdrive. He climbed to the construction site and stood before the half finished structure.

Whispers came from the shadows. They spoke of death, pain and suffering. The voices taunted him with his deepest fears and promised oblivion if he would come inside and join them.

He steeled himself and began to pour the cans of kerosene and lamp oil he had brought with him around the front of the house, careful not to splash any on his clothes.

The dry wood soaked up the liquid. The voices rose, warning him of what would happen if he continued. He ignored them all and lit a small lamp that held more oil. The wick flared and he threw the glass against the base of the front door. The fire shot up and around, eagerly following the fuel's path.

He waited, watching the house until everything that could burn was alit. Bright yellow flames reached their tendrils to the night sky. Sparks flew, swirling into the air—some individually, some like a cloud of insects. The voices changed from cajoling to pleading to stop. Others joined in as the wood charred and split, the sound growing in intensity until the air was filled with the wails and howls of a multitude of voices, each a separate cadence and tone.

On top of the natural orange fire Viktor was used to, blue hues began to appear here and there until there were hundreds of the luminescent lights—one for each *trapped spirit*, he surmised. They gave off a strange tingling sensation like Saint Elmo's fire. Whatever this was, it was different than that. This burned with an unnatural light—Hellfire.

The rain started as a light drizzle and then turned into a downpour. Through it all the fire burned and Viktor stood guard.

Mist rose after the thunderstorm ceased. Its vapor twisted and mingled with the smoke from the smoldering ruins. Viktor looked over the cliffs and down at the waves crashing onto the beach. He turned his gaze towards the village and saw the faint glow of lanterns and torches as people made their way to the cliff. Seamus had done his job well and kept the town people away from the danger.

Under the waters, farther out, the sea glowed with an unnatural green light deep below the swells until the rolling fog covered it. Every direction was closing in on him it seemed. Mist. Smoke. Fog. The faint glow of the rising sun only added to the surreal scene. The atmosphere would have scared him at an earlier time, but after the events of the past few months it filled him instead with grim determination.

He vowed there and then to finish the job, find all the pieces of wood that might contain more of the spirits. They were out there. He couldn't leave the village knowing what he knew. There must be others of like mind out there, and he would be patient and find them. Together they would protect the residents from whatever lurked in the shadows. Something must have attracted them to this location, and he would do whatever it took to find out what it was.

He sat on edge of the cliff and waited for the villagers to arrive and knew this was only the first of many nights he would hold vigil over some evil.

The Present

"And that's how the Shadow Keepers got started. Viktor led a long and exciting life, keeping as many safe as he could from the demons and dominions that made the village and what later became Shadow Street such a seething cesspool of paranormal activity. He never did find out about the real cause — no one had, until you and I went to Hell a few months ago. But, now we know and we will have to face that issue soon with Thomas."

I looked up at Death but he was gazing thoughtfully at Merrick, so I did, too. His eyes were wide and fearful, and he kept glancing over my shoulder at the woods. He sat with his arms around Smokie who was completely knocked out.

Probably couldn't handle the sudden withdrawal of sugar.

Death had finished his story but the sensation that had started while he told his story continued to grow rather than abate. I couldn't quell the feelings inside and my heart started beating faster and faster. Something was wrong. Very wrong.

I stopped myself from looking behind me, into the pitch-black depths of the forest. It was only Death's story that caused my spooky feelings. I spent a minute trying to convince myself of that, but I was fooling only myself. I knew something lurked in that stygian darkness, and I stood and turned in almost one motion, shrugging Death's arm from my shoulders as I did.

"What is it, Beka? What's wrong? It was just a story that happened years ago."

"No. No, it wasn't," I replied, as sure of this as the fact that Smokie would want another candy bar the second he woke. "Something is out there. Something is waiting for us."

In a second, Death stood, his massive back in my face, causing me to take a half step back.

"I'm not entirely helpless, you know," I said between clenched teeth.

"I know that, but let me…"

"Let you what? Be the man? Really? Are we going to have this conversation?"

"Um…no?" For the first time that I had known him, Death sounded wary and cautious. "Forget I even started to say that, please. I forgot myself for a moment."

Hiding a small smile—sorry women's lib, it was nice for a second having a feeling that the big strong male wanted to protect little old me—I pushed him over a bit so we could stand side by side and face whatever was out there together. Heat at my other side let me know Smokie was up and alert as well, standing guard next to us. Merrick moved to his other side, looking a bit puzzled. Oh well, I sighed to myself. I could fight their need to flank and protect me or just be happy that they cared enough to worry and have my back. I decided just to be happy.

It's not moving," I said. "It's waiting for something to happen. It needs us. I'm not even sure what *it* is."

I opened my senses to the night and knew Death was doing the same. I startled when I felt those first tentative probes from my other side. Merrick? He was about the right age. The sensation I felt from him was not like anything I had felt for a long time. This was going to get very complicated very quickly. He and I were going to have to have a little talk. Then my attention was captured as I felt other emotions rolling over me— hatred, anger, the pure unadulterated need to kill. They were tinged with a wildness that was half human and half animal. It was similar to the Minotaur. But, it couldn't be. It was back where it needed to be. This entity hungered with a need to be free, to feed, to ravage, and to rend. It wanted blood. It wanted our fear. I couldn't get a fix on it though. It was almost as if it surrounded us. As if…

I jumped back, one hand on Death's arm dragging him with me, another on the collar of Merrick's shirt. I pushed and pulled them until we stood on the other side of the fire, away from that large log we had been leaning against.

Inside of me, I knew. I knew what we had been next to this whole time. The whole time Death had told us that scary tale.

A deep growl told me Smokie sensed something, too. I put my hand on his back and smoothed his hackles, but his fur immediately rose again. He was in no mood to be placated or soothed.

"Beka, get back farther. You know what that is, too, don't you?"

"We have to burn it like Viktor burned the house. It can't be allowed to stay here. It's getting stronger for some reason. It wants out, and it wants blood. Ours to start. We have to either kill it or send it back."

"I'm kind of partial to where my blood is at the moment, thank you very much," Death said.

"Smokie, guard Merrick. Go." I pointed at Merrick, and I swear for a moment Smokie's eyes flashed the clear red of Hell's fire.

"Aww, Beka. I can help. I know I can. I'm just like you."

"No, Merrick, you are not just like me. You're something different, but that's a topic for another night. You need to stay back and safe for now. This is not a game."

To give Merrick his due, he stayed quiet and moved, Smokie at his side. I could tell by the trembling in Smokie's body that he was anxious to get in on the action, but I needed Merrick safe and Smokie stood guard.

Death and I bent and each of us grabbed a burning stick from the campfire. I moved close enough to the tree trunk we had been leaning against to set the stick to the top of it, and Death did the same. We repeated that gesture time and time again, burning our hands several times in the process. The trunk caught fire. Eerie blue flames scattered over and around the wood until the entire length was a mass of swirling light and dark blue—Hellfire—beautiful in its intensity. The electricity in it crackled and sent the hairs on my head and arms on end.

A low-pitched howl rent the night, growing until I had to clap my hands over my ears. I looked at Death and saw him mouth something to me, but I couldn't understand him. With a thunderous crash, the trunk split from tip to stern and out rose a monster. Half man, half goat, he towered over Death's tall form. It had been trapped in the figurehead all these years, and it was overjoyed at being released. Overjoyed with the destruction it could bring. Its gaze was hot and feverish and there was a glint of madness in its eyes. It stood, trapped within the blue flames, unable to step out for the moment. The smell of sulfur and brimstone filled my nostrils. It was a smell I had so recently inhaled more than my fill of and it made me sick to my stomach.

"You," it said looking at Death. "Of all to free me, it is you. Who is this small pink person next to you? She will be fun to play with once I kill you."

"I wondered what happened to you, Deimos. You ran away like a little child, leaving your comrades to face me alone. They died knowing they were lost forever having followed a weak coward."

"Come and see how weak of a coward I am. When I am done, I will feast on the bones of this small female."

"Hellooo," I said, waving my hand to get their attention. "Stop talking over me. I can take care of myself, Mr. Short, Red, and Ugly."

Death laughed. Deimos snarled. It was all too much for Smokie. With a large howl, he leapt forward and onto the demon. His forelegs stretched out and connected with its chest. A flash of light, another roar of thunder and *poof*, they vanished. The blue flames continued to burn for a second and then they too were gone, only the light of the campfire was left. For a moment, there was dead silence.

"Smokie! No. No. Come back." I was almost sobbing in fear.

"Where did they go, Beka? You have to know. We need to get Smokie back." Merrick ran over and stood next to me. He looked as anxious as I felt.

"They went to seventh circle of Hell. We can't enter, not yet. They will be waiting for us," Death held my arm, stopping me from running to the split tree.

I turned to face him, frantic with worry. "We don't have to. I can bring Smokie back. I can cast a spell."

"If you do that you'll bring the demon back also. You know anything in Smokie's proximity will return with him. We can't risk that."

"Are you suggesting we just leave Smokie there?"

"Well, he is a Hellhound. It is home for him."

"I'll discuss that comment with you later when we have more time. Smokie doesn't belong there anymore. You know that. He made his choice. He's ours, not theirs."

"Hey, don't get mad at me. I was merely making an observation. I'm as worried about the beast as you are. I'm thinking. I'm thinking."

"I know how," Merrick said suddenly. "One second." He reached into the picnic hamper and picked up a candy bar. Opening the wrapper he crinkled the foil in one hand and whistled. "Here, Smokie. Come and get it."

Barely had the last word left his mouth when a flurry of sparks rose from the campfire and Smokie stood in the ash and smoke, his eyes a terrible red at first before they faded to their usual ice-blue flames. He ignored the candy and came over to me and sat, staring up into my face.

I couldn't help it. I went to my knees and wrapped my arms around him and sobbed in relief. I loved the beast. Death placed one hand on my head, and I could feel him rubbing the loose folds of skin around Smokie's neck with his other. Smokie's hot body pressed close to me, and I could feel the heated chuffs of his breath against my neck.

That lasted a whole fifteen seconds.

One more crinkle of the candy bar's wrapper and Smokie was at Merrick's side, happily chewing on the Whatchamacallit. Our Hallmark moment was over, but my heart wouldn't stop beating hard. Death pulled me up and wrapped his arms around me, my back to his chest.

I took a moment to enjoy the warmth of his arms and the comfort he gave.

"You're going to have to tell me about this interesting past you have, someday," I said to him and snuggled back a bit firmer, happy for his warmth.

"I'll tell you someday when we're having a lazy night by the fire, and no demons are lurking around."

I made a half laugh, half sob sound. Seeing Smokie licking his chops from the candy bar made me relieved. So relieved, I decided to make a clean break of it all.

"There is one issue I haven't had the guts to tell you about," I said, pulling away and facing him, my eyes still damp from the recent fear. "It's about the prom. I can't find a thing to wear. Can't we stay home and watch a movie with Uncle Jasper?"

"I swear you have no female genes in you, Beka. Most women would kill to go shopping. Don't worry, I know just the person that would go with you. Alison will help."

"Do I know her? I don't think so."

"Let's just say she knows you, and she'll love it. Who knows, she may even teach you to enjoy it."

I snorted in disbelief. "What's next? Puppies and rainbows?"

At that moment there was another *poof,* and we turned to look at the campfire.

A smaller, sleeker, reddish version of Smokie stood in the flames—by the looks of it a female Hellhound.

Smokie bounded over and the two touched noses for a second in some silent communication before racing along the sandy beach. Within a few moments, the sounds of fowl squawking in the night air could be heard.

My mind expanded to other possibilities. Oh. My. God. No, no, no.

"No puppies. Oh, please. No puppies. How will I ever explain that?"

Death and Merrick started howling with laughter.

I sighed.

Nothing is ever easy on Shadow Street.

DARKNESS
Somewhere Underground
by Morgan Ashe

"You really shouldn't be mad at him, Beka. It really was just an accident." Death spoke to me in that quiet, reasonable sounding voice that immediately set my mad at an even higher level.

"Have you ever noticed that everything with that crazy Hellhound is just an accident," I asked with a tone in my voice that even Death could not ignore. "We've had the Peanut Butter Incident, the Feathered Fowl Incident, the Outdoor Chocolatier's Demonstration Incident, and that's only a few. Every time I turn around that hound is into something." I almost cringed at the sound of the whine in my voice. It was two days before the prom, and I was having panic attacks. What if Death didn't like my dress? What if I tripped in my new shoes? Who really wore 4-inch heels? I was insane for buying them but they were the prettiest black leather with cold iron heels and a cold iron buckle. They might not be traditional prom shoes, but they were badass. The minute I saw them I knew I had to have them. If all else failed and I lost my dagger, I could impale something on them. I had actually had a good time shopping with Alison, but I didn't think I'd ever find the same love for shoes that she had. Thinking that happy thought, I calmed myself and even sat up straighter as if being taller while seated would make me sound more in charge.

In charge. That was funny. Death and I were at the bottom of a fifteen-foot hole in the ground. Thank goodness it was sandy or one of us would have broken something. As it was, Death cushioned my fall. Good thing he wasn't technically alive. One problem was it was dark outside thanks to Shadow Street's Dusky Moon phase and neither one of our flashlights had survived the drop so we couldn't see the top of the hole. Note to self—get some flashlights that can survive Hellhound incidents.

The second problem was that something was suppressing our powers. I could barely draw enough to light a small blue witch fire. It was able to show a small tunnel that neither Death nor I felt inclined to start exploring. Smokie had gone on ahead and for the moment I was happy to just sit and try to regain my equilibrium after the fall.

"Where are we anyway? I didn't know there was a hole around here—or caves for that matter. I'm assuming that's where that wretch has disappeared. Probably looking for a snack. As if the three he's had in the last hour weren't enough."

"Well, he is a growing Hellhound. Those fowl were just an appetizer, I'm sure," he said, again in that reasonable sounding tone. My mad was approaching eruption point.

"Does the fact that we are sitting here fifteen feet underground in the pitch dark with a hungry Hellhound roaming around and no idea of what was stalking us have any meaning to you?" I asked. "Or are we going to sit here and make excuses for him instead?"

"Well, in his defense, he was trying to get us away from whatever that was. It must have worked since it didn't follow us down here."

"That we know of. How would we know? We can barely see ourselves in here let alone a monster. I'm not even convinced something or someone was stalking us. We still don't know where Heli has been hiding. Or any of the members of the Cult of Destiny's Shadow. You know we really have to figure out where they are meeting. All I saw was a little glow in one direction and then Smokie running like an idiot past us. He was... Can you smell that?" I interrupted myself as something that smelled like wet feathers began to waft its way across my olfactory senses and, it was getting stronger.

"Do you smell that?"

"I was trying to ignore it, actually."

Suddenly, a large raucous clucking sounded and then began to get louder—if that were possible I thought. Smokie came first. His glowing eyes and the faintly visible runes of the same ice blue were a dead give away, but didn't explain the small turquoise glow behind him. He barreled into me and actually tried to squeeze behind myself and the dirt wall I had been leaning against.

The smell of wet feathers got stronger and stronger and then, much to my amazement, Death's amusement, and Smokie's terror, the turquoise light formed into a large...chicken.

"I'm sorry," I began. "Is that...that a chicken?"

"Oh, it's a chicken all right." Death wheezed in air between gasps of laughter. "A slightly dead, ghost chicken."

"It's one of those mutant chickens from the woods. Smokie, I told you to leave them alone. You have got to stop eating those chickens. Now they are learning to come back and haunt you. This is your entire fault. Again." I couldn't believe how Smokie was shaking against me and trying to burrow under my jacket as if to hide from the furious ghost fowl.

"Aww, Beka. A Hellhound has to have some fun."

Meanwhile, the chicken was standing at the mouth of the small cave squawking and flapping its wings. The overwhelming smell of wet feathers was really starting to give me a headache. *How can a dead chicken stink?* I wondered.

"Well, do something," I said to Death who was still laughing like a fool. "You take care of this since you're on Smokie's side."

"Do what? If it were real, I could roast it I suppose. I am feeling hungry."

"Don't be more of an idiot than Smokie is right now. It's late. I'm tired. And I have a headache."

"Anything I can do to help?" The words seemed to float down from above.

Looking up, I could only see a light shining. Fortunately, I knew Thomas' voice.

"Yeah, first of all, don't fall in. This place is already cramped and one more..." I began only to be interrupted again by the ghost chicken. It ran around frantically and then abruptly vanished.

"Where did it go?" I asked.

"Hopefully to whatever fowl heaven there is," Death said. "Hey, Thomas. How about a hand?" Something is causing a bit of an issue with our powers down here. Something we'll have to look into, I suspect."

In a flash, all three of us were standing next to Thomas. "We can look into it later," Thomas said. "I have a meeting with the Guardian Council in an hour and I am afraid I'll need both of you to come with me. They are getting rid of Jackson as head of the Shadow Keepers."

I watched Death stare at Thomas and Thomas stare at Death. Some silent communication seemed to be taking place.

"What's going on? I asked. "What is happening with Jackson? He's been around for an eternity."

"Oh nothing," Thomas said. "Just several little screw ups over the past few months. First there was the entire Inanna mishap, then the Lysovik.

The Guardians aren't very happy with him right now. But don't worry, they have someone in mind."

I was distracted as Smokie went over to look down into the pit. *Probably praying... do Hellhounds pray?... that he wouldn't see any flashes of blue,* I thought. He pricked his ears up at some sound too quiet or high pitched for me to hear and then went off into the bushes. I sighed. It was going to be a long night.

"You know, Beka. This may be one for the records. We could have the first recorded ghost chicken." Death grinned at me and kissed me gently on the nose. "Don't look so mad. All in all it was another interesting evening."

I stuck my tongue out at him and began to move towards the path to get back to the top of the cliffs.

"Hey, Beka." Thomas came up beside me and draped an arm across my shoulders. "Do you know what they call a ghost chicken?"

"Seriously? Jokes at this time?" I asked. Finally, giving in to his pouting face, I responded. "No, Thomas. What do you call a ghost chicken?

"Why a poultry-geist, of course."

I rolled my eyes, pulled away from him, and turned to see him and Death laughing like a pair of hyenas. "Really, you two need help. Major help."

I started walking up the hill only to stop and turn as I heard the ominous sounds of clucking. Racing out of the bushes was Smokie with feathers still fluttering around his mouth and face. He pranced over to where Death and Thomas were laughing and sat facing them. Each time they looked at him they started laughing again. The Hellhound was grinning like an idiot, his mouth open with a long pink tongue poked out between sharp white teeth. He looked like a cat that had just eaten a canary. Or, in this case, a Hellhound who had just eaten a mutant chicken.

"You three deserve each other," I said crossly. Then couldn't help it and started laughing. A night of ghost chickens was one to remember.

Part III

Now for Something Completely Different...

DEMETER'S DAY OUT
Backroads of Shadow Street
by Denise Vitola

"This stupid GPS is useless. It doesn't work on Shadow Street. I thought you were going to have it recalibrated, because of the fiasco that happened the last time."

"Hush, Persephone. I never said I needed that infernal machine. I can find the Omphalos without it. I've been hiding it since before you were born. Besides, you just can't have people stumbling around and finding the Womb of the World—even here. They could mash a wrong button and then things could get complicated. I might miss a nail appointment to deal with something like that. It's just not worth it."

"But would it have killed you to keep this one alley swept clean? No, you have to make everything bloom everywhere—even trash. By Chaos, I've never seen so much litter."

"I'm Demeter, the Goddess of Rebirth. It's my job to make things spring forth, in abandon and profusion—even trash. This is the best I can do in this time slip. Flowers and sunny hillsides are few and far between here. And honestly, I didn't want to put the opening in the middle of a swamp."

"What is that? A rat? Oh my god, it's a rat. With six legs. And he's huge. Who, in their right mind, would create such a monstrosity?"

"Probably Hera. She's rather fond of diddling with DNA. You recall the brouhaha with the three-headed Hydra. Hercules never did live that one down."

"Why don't you save us some time and ask the Angel-in-Charge where you hid the opening? I'm sure he knows everything. He acts like he does, anyway."

"Oh, he's a handsome one, isn't he? Dark and brooding. Just my kind of man. Angel. Whatever. Don't tell Zeus I said that. With his jealousy, we could have a misunderstanding of epic proportions."

"Mother, you're stalling. You unlocked the Womb less than six months ago and now you can't remember where you stashed the hatch."

"Speaking of six months ago, have you heard from that creep you call a husband?"

"Hades is not a creep, Mother."

"Darling, you have Stockholm Syndrome. Do you know what that is?"

"No, but I expect you'll tell me."

"It's when you fall in love with your kidnapper."

"He didn't kidnap me. I ate that wormy apple and then I had to stay. You know that."

"Yes, and I told you to keep to a low-carb diet, but no. You had to have a piece of fruit. Would it have killed you to wait until you were back on Mt. Olympus before you got a sugar fix?"

"You're trying to change the subject. We're talking about you not being able to change the seasons to autumn and winter until you can find the Omphalos. Summer is getting to be a drag, Mother. The humidity is messing with my hair. Especially here."

"Well, I know the trapdoor is around here somewhere. That little electronic nightmare you're holding is confirming it. Stop blaming the weather instead of your no-talent hairdresser and listen."

Proceed two meters.

"It's that lousy British accent. Why do they have to tune these things that way?"

You are here.

"Where?"

"Kick that garbage away from in front of those overflowing dumpsters."

"Are you serious? These shoes are Dolce and Gabbana. No, Mother. You let it profuse; you move it."

"Honestly, Persephone. You get on my last nerve sometimes. Wait, there it is."

"Open it so you can lock down the season. I'm ready to get out of here. Shadow Street is…disturbing. I think I saw a half-Human-half-Hog walking down the street carrying a cat under his arm."

"They're called Hybrids, my dear, and that wasn't a cat. It was a *Fumus*. Hybrids are creatures birthed by Zeus when he beds handmaidens and queens. The Guardians of Eternity indulge him because he's king of the Greek gods, but they don't want his rather odd children mixing with the general Human population back on Earth anymore. That's why they're packing them down on Shadow Street. Besides, the Hybrids are no different than satyrs. And if I remember correctly, you never had a problem with those cloven footed reprobates."

"Mother, my sex life is none of your business. Put the key in the lock, twist the dials, and let's blow this joint."

"Hang on a minute. The lock got a little rusty. I suppose I sent too much rain this past spring."

"Hades is waiting for me."

"Have a little patience, dear, will you? All you have to do is go back down and stare at the zombies while he makes pronouncements over their fates. Why don't you join Zeus and me in Rio? It's wonderful in the winter."

"You know I can't, Mother. Besides, Father hates my husband."

"Who said anything about bringing him along?"

"Mother."

"All right. All right. Well, if you won't come to party with us, tell me when you and the big Lord of the Underworld are going to have children. It's been, what, 5,000 years? It's time you started a family. I'm not getting any younger, you know."

AUTHOR BIOS

Morgan Ashe — Morgan decided long ago that her version of reality was much better than actual reality. As such, everything you read in her stories is true in her plane of existence. She moved to Shadow Street in the early 1600s to avoid being burned at the stake. Although she wasn't a witch, her stories were deemed inappropriate for the times and she spent many a night avoiding angry villagers carrying pitchforks and torches. Her life in Shadow Street has been much quieter even though her next-door neighbor is a ghost who regularly bugs her for a cup of ectoplasm. Now, if she can just figure out who keeps chasing her chickens.

She can be reached at ashe@morganashe.com or her website at morganashe.com.

Denise Vitola — Denise blends esoteric ideas with myth, legend, and mystery to create worlds where the impossible seems possible. Her novel, OPALITE MOON, the second in her popular Ty Merrick Mystery series, was nominated for the prestigious Philip K. Dick Award for Excellence in Science Fiction. This series was optioned by Universal Studios to be made into a television show. When not writing and communing with the Angel Thomas, she can be found sitting behind a pair of knitting needles, determined to make a scarf long enough to wrap around the entire planet.

She can be reached at denise@mygrande.net or her website at thomas-talks-to-me.com